KISS ME

VAMPIRE BRIDE BOOK 3

LINSEY HALL

1

Mac

I'd struck out. Again.

The door to the Mage's Coffee Shop slammed behind me as I stepped out onto the street. Early autumn wind blew my hair back from my face and cleared my head of the scents of cappuccino and scones.

Even the bright sunlight couldn't cheer me up. The Mind Mage that I'd just visited was the most powerful in town. Since I had a little bit of my real memory left, I'd hoped she could maybe help me remember more.

Nope.

I was still clueless about my past.

Still had no idea who had erased my memory. The bits and pieces that I knew had been stitched together haphazardly, leaving massive blank spots I had no idea how to fill.

My attempts to find answers over the last couple days had proven fruitless, and this most recent trip was no exception.

I leaned against an iron lamp post and sighed. All around, people bustled along in front of Guild City's quaint shops. There was a cheerful energy in the air that usually accompanied the beginning of a nice day, but I couldn't appreciate it.

As I stepped out into the cobblestone street, thoughts of my mother flashed in my mind. I hadn't seen her since the dream two days ago, but now that I'd gotten a glimpse of her face, I'd become obsessed.

As if thinking of her had triggered a connection, the world seemed to fade away. The cool breeze disappeared, along with the sound of shoppers and motorbikes zipping along the street.

Suddenly, I was trapped within my mind. All around, tall stone walls closed in on me. The air smelled damp and stale, and very little light filtered through the space.

A tomb?

A castle?

"Daughter."

The voice sounded from behind, and I whirled, heart pounding. "Mother."

She stood in front of me, identical to how I'd seen

her in my dream. Same green cloak and pale, wispy hair drawn up into an elegant knot. The fine lines around her face only served to make her more beautiful, and my heart pounded as I looked at her.

"What's happening?"

"Now that you've remembered me, we're connected through our minds."

"Did I get my power from you? What *is* it?" She'd told me that I had the power of creation, but I wasn't sure exactly what that meant. I knew I wasn't a conjurer, not in the traditional sense.

"No, daughter. As I told you before, you are truly unique. Your magic is of your mind, a power that only you possess."

"That's so unclear." Frustration surged within me. "I need more information."

"Come save me, and you will have it."

"Save you?"

Her form wavered, turning slightly transparent, and her brow creased as worry flickered in her eyes. "Hurry. I am trapped. Only you can find me."

I reached out for her, heart pounding, but she disappeared.

A horn blared and shouts sounded. The world seemed to spin around me, blurry and strange, making it impossible for my vision to focus. Something hit me in the back and shoved me out of the road. My vision cleared right before I slammed into one of the ancient trees planted in front of a potion shop, and I threw up my hands to protect my face.

Panting, I rested against the bark. A heavy weight clung to my back, but I knew without looking that it was Genevieve, my badger familiar, clinging to the shoulders of my leather jacket.

I never took you for a tree hugger. Her voice sounded right at my ear, and I turned my head slightly to look at her.

"The environment has always been very important to me." Panting, I pushed myself off the tree, and she hopped down from my back. When I turned to look at the street, I spotted an angry man on a motorbike glaring at me.

You were standing in the middle of the road like a ninny.

"Yeah. That was weird." I gave an apologetic wave, and the man revved his little engine and moved on.

What the hell had just happened?

Care to explain yourself?

I looked down at Genevieve, who'd hauled herself up onto a pretty iron bench that sat beneath the tree. She had a rhinestone bow clipped to the fur above her ear, which was a new look for her, but I didn't ask about it.

"I had a vision of my mother." I pinched the bridge of my nose. "The first since the dream two nights ago."

Why the visions suddenly? She's been missing from your memory for years.

"She said it's because I've started to remember her. She needs me to find her."

Where is she?

"No idea." My gaze sharpened on Genevieve as the shock wore off and I remembered why Genevieve wore a rhinestone in her fur. "Did you find Drakon?"

Yes. Although he didn't see me. She patted the rhinestone on her furry head and sounded a bit peeved. My badger familiar had developed a bit of a crush on the vampire, and the rhinestone bow was the likely result of her infatuation.

"Where is he?"

Vegas. Her eyes lit up. *Now* there's *a fun place.*

"Vegas? What the hell is he doing in Vegas?"

Not playing the slots, which is what I'd be doing. She shrugged. *Otherwise, I have no idea. As soon as I saw him, I came to tell you immediately, just like you asked.*

"Thank you." It had been two days since he'd slammed the door in my face, and I was worried about him. I knew a future between us was impossible, but he was still cursed, his soul slowly becoming entombed in granite. We didn't have long before the curse became permanent, and I couldn't get him out of my mind. "I've got to go find him."

Genevieve's eyes brightened. *Perfect. I'll come with.*

"To see Drakon?"

To play the slots. And to see if the casino makes a decent Manhattan. She gave a toothy grin. She was fascinated with Drakon, but she might love slot machines more.

My badger familiar was a posh old lady with a fondness for strong whiskey cocktails and slot machines. How had I gotten so lucky?

"I have a transport charm. Can you lead me to him?"

Genevieve hopped off the bench. *But of course. I am Genevieve. I can do anything.*

Drakon

Humans. So many damned humans.

Vegas was a cesspool of the creatures, and this casino was no exception. The building was a massive place, entirely done up in sleek black stone and bright silver metal. Fountains shot sparkling water into the air between the gambling tables and slot machines. Acrobats dangled from the ceiling by silken cloths, spinning and twirling beneath the glittering lights.

All around, humans gambled away their savings, drinking and laughing. Vague distaste filled me, along with a ravenous hunger that ate at my bones.

Normally, this might have been a buffet of endless options.

Now, I craved only Mac.

I'd tried drinking from other people, but their blood had just made me ill. It certainly hadn't forestalled any part of the curse that currently stalked me. A taste of Mac's blood had bought me several days, but I could still feel my fate dogging at my heels, sinking its teeth into me.

She was the only cure, and there was no way I'd ever tell her. She deserved better.

The energy in the air was stained with excitement and desperation, only one of which I shared. All it did was serve to remind me that I felt more dead than I had since I'd been created.

I shoved away the miserable thoughts and strode through the crowd. People parted to let me pass, several of them dropping their handfuls of chips as I moved by them. Humans didn't know what I was, but they recognized a predator in their midst.

I passed card games and roulette, slots and dice, my gaze fixed on the doors on the far side of the room. Four suit-clad men stood at the entrance, their arms crossed in front of them as they stared stonily at the casino floor.

Guards.

They stood between me and the elevator that would take me to one of the most powerful seers in the world. Orinthia had decided to run a human casino in Vegas, and it baffled me. The money would be excellent, of course, but there were far more pleasant ways for a seer to make money.

The four guards stiffened as I approached, their eyes turning wary.

Good.

I wished this damned casino weren't full of humans. If it were only supernaturals, I could fight my way through. That wouldn't be the quickest way, but it would be the most satisfying.

Here, that would just cause a scene I didn't need.

Unfortunately, the guards were human.

No matter.

I could just compel them. It was easier than fighting, though far less enjoyable. As I stopped in front of them, the elevator doors at their backs whizzed open silently.

A small man stood within, eyes bright and face set in a worried smile. His magic smelled faintly of ink, like an old book.

Good. A supernatural. Finally.

"Move aside, move aside." He pushed at the shoulders of the guards who still blocked the entrance to the elevator. "You might be too stupid to know who this is, but I am not. Let him pass."

The biggest guard turned to him. "The boss approves?"

"Of course, you imbecile. Now let Drakon pass."

The guards huffed and stepped aside.

I ignored them as I entered the elevator. The man moved over to give me space, then pressed the button for the top floor. "I saw you arrive through the security cameras. To what do we owe the honor?"

"I need to see your boss."

"But of course. She'd be delighted to have a meeting with you." He pulled out a slender book and flipped to a page that showed the days of the week.

"Now." The ice in my voice made him flinch, and he quickly flipped the book closed and tucked it into his pocket. "Of course."

The elevator rose silently and swiftly. The glass-walled capsule was located at the side of the building, providing an expansive view of the entire Vegas strip. Millions of lights glittered outside, an oasis of human sin in the middle of the desert.

"Amazing, isn't it?" the man asked.

"Hmm." The view could have revealed a spaceship from Mars and I wouldn't have cared. I had only two things on my mind--finding a cure and Mac.

The only cure I knew of was to drink her blood daily. That was hardly an option for me. It wasn't a life she would want, and it wasn't one I wanted either. I didn't want to be bound to someone—particularly the one person who had the power to take away my immortality.

Not that she knew that.

In fact, it wasn't even *her* who could take it away.

It would be me, falling for her and igniting the Bride Prophecy.

And that was unacceptable. After so many centuries

alive, I couldn't resign myself to the idea that I would become mortal and die in sixty years.

There had to be another way.

The elevator doors whooshed open silently, revealing a massive office that took up the entire top floor. The glass walls provided a view of the glittering strip and the dark desert beyond. A large, gleaming wooden desk sat in the middle of the space.

The woman behind it lounged with the relaxed grace of a queen, confident that her kingdom was secure. Next to her sat a tiger, and it was immediately apparent that the beast was a shifter. It purred loudly, emerald eyes glinting.

"Drakon." Her voice echoed with boredom, just enough that I was certain it was an affectation.

Orinthia was interested in the fact that I was here.

Good.

Hopefully, that would make her more inclined to help me. I could always compel her, but that was never guaranteed to work, and willing assistance was always worth more.

"Orinthia. It's been a long time."

She rose and strode around the desk. Her glittering gold dress draped to the floor, a sleek silhouette that made her look like a golden statue. Objectively, she was a beautiful woman, with dark hair and green eyes, and once upon a time, I might have seduced her into giving me what I wanted.

Now, I couldn't have been less interested in that tactic.

Hell, I felt incapable of it.

Mac had ruined me for any other woman, so I'd have to do this the old-fashioned way.

Bribery.

She leaned against the front of the desk. "To what do I owe this magnificent pleasure?"

I stopped about ten feet in front of her. "I'd like to secure your services as a seer."

"Sorry, I don't do that anymore."

"Too busy with the humans down below?"

She smiled. "Humans are delightful. They are so easy to manipulate. And frankly, a seer can make a lot of money in a place like Vegas."

"Cheating pays."

"Everyone's a cheater. I'm just better at it." She smiled. "The best, really."

"You're also one of the best seers, and I need your help. I'll pay you whatever you want."

"A night with you."

"Not that."

She clucked her tongue, but she didn't look surprised. "I did think you seemed different."

"I'm turning to stone, so let's say I'm not in the mood."

"Oh, I'd say that means you're in *just* the right mood."

If I were the sort to roll my eyes, they'd have been at the back of my head. "Literally, I mean. And I need a cure."

She sighed. "For old time's sake and a million dollars, I'll do my best."

"How generous." It wasn't a bad price, actually. At least, not for someone of her skill level and my resources. Being alive so long made it easy to accumulate wealth. "I'll have it transferred as soon as we're done."

"Good." She smiled and gestured me closer. "Now, come here."

I strode toward her, stopping a couple of feet in front of her and breathing shallowly to avoid taking in too much of her cloying perfume.

"Hold out a hand."

I did as she commanded, and she rested her fingertips on the back of my hand. Despite her invitation to pay her in bed, she made a point to touch me as little as possible.

At her side, the tiger growled, its glowing eyes on us.

"Down boy," she murmured.

The tiger huffed but didn't look away as her magic flared on the air. The scent of cinnamon and the taste of apples hit me before she dropped her hand and stepped back.

"There's nothing I can do for you." Her voice was flat

and final. "You already have the only answer you're ever going to get."

"Mac."

"Is that her name?"

I nodded.

"Yes, then. Mac. You know she's your cure, and yet you're still here paying me a *million dollars* to confirm it?"

"Essentially." As much as I was determined to find another way, I knew there probably wasn't one. Orinthia was a powerful seer, powerful enough to get to the bottom of that. I'd *hoped* she'd have information about another cure for me, but I'd accepted that the most I might get out of this meeting was confirmation that Mac was the only way.

Which meant there was no way.

Orinthia clucked her tongue. "You shouldn't give up so fast. You might find her more willing to help than you think."

"Even if she did, drinking her blood every day would be a bond I couldn't escape. I'd lose my immortality."

"Hmm. Another part of the Bride Prophecy?"

"Yes. You saw quite a lot while you were in there, didn't you?"

"I'm a quick worker. The best for a reason." She nodded toward something behind me. "But just because *I* can't help you, doesn't mean no one can."

Awareness shivered down my spine, and suddenly I could feel someone's gaze on me.

Mac.

"She's here, isn't she?"

"Standing behind the glass doors that lead to my balcony, staring in like a stalker."

I turned to see her standing exactly as Orinthia had described, though I wouldn't have labeled her a stalker.

Beautiful.

Intriguing.

Powerful.

But not a stalker.

Or if she was, I didn't mind.

No. Of course I minded. I couldn't have anything to do with her.

"I'll leave you to it." Orinthia pushed herself up off the desk and clicked her fingers. The tiger gave an annoyed huff but stood and followed her toward the elevator. As the doors whooshed open, Orinthia turned back to me and raised her brows. "There are no security cameras up here. You know, just in case."

Before I could respond, she disappeared into the elevator. I turned and strode toward the balcony doors, sliding one open.

The warm desert breeze rushed in, bringing Mac's intoxicating scent along with it. I resisted drawing it deeply into my lungs but couldn't keep my eyes from racing over her face. Looking at her felt like a balm to the soul, and every inch of my body ached to pull her into my arms.

It had been two long days since I'd shut the door in her face, and the memory of the desperate kiss we'd shared just before still haunted me.

"What are you doing here?" I asked.

"What are *you* doing here?" Her gaze moved to the elevator where Orinthia had disappeared. "New girlfriend?"

"Jealous?"

"Kind of." She scowled. "Which is annoying as hell because I'm never jealous."

I wished I hadn't asked. It just reminded me of how much there was between us that I didn't want to think about. Couldn't afford to think about. Because if I spent even a moment focused on her, I wanted nothing more than to pull her into my arms and forget everything.

2

Mac

I stared at Drakon, my heart racing. The tension between us was so thick that I almost couldn't breathe.

Underneath the desert moonlight, he looked like a conquering warrior. Power radiated from him, ancient and invisible. Though I knew I shouldn't look at his lips, I couldn't help myself. Memories of our kisses flashed through my mind, heating up my soul until I might burst into flame.

I'm going to go win some money. This is getting weird. Genevieve disappeared.

I looked at Drakon. "Why are you here?"

"Looking for a cure."

"There really wasn't one in the book that I gave you?"

"Nothing." His gaze moved over my shoulder.

Suspicion flickered through me. "You're lying."

His eyes snapped back to mine. "I'm not. There was nothing in the book that would work."

There was such conviction in his voice that I almost believed him. Almost.

"You're holding something back."

"I'm holding a lot of things back, Mac. You know I can't trust you, not after you locked me in that tomb."

I winced, unable to argue. I *had* done that, and I now had the memories to prove it. They were hazy and didn't include *why* I'd done it, but I knew I had.

And he no doubt hated me for it. Didn't trust me.

So I should count myself lucky that he'd told me this much truth. But I still wanted more, and I knew there was something here that he wasn't sharing. "I can help you, Drakon. I want to."

"You can't."

Lie. The instinct rushed through me. He was lying. Quickly, I reached out and gripped his arm, hoping to get a feeling for the truth. Heat zinged through me where we touched, then a stab of pain.

It came from him. *He* was feeling that chest tightening sensation of turning to stone, and I could feel it as long as I touched him.

He stiffened and pulled back. "Don't even try it."

Annoyance surged through me, and I scowled at him. "Whatever you're hiding, I'll figure it out."

He just grunted.

Absently, I rubbed my chest. It still hurt, as if the memory of his pain had imprinted on me.

"Are you all right?" he asked.

"Fine." I turned to look out at the glittering lights of the city, barely noticing the cool breeze that brushed my hair back. "Just need to figure out my next step."

He hesitated briefly before speaking, as if fighting the desire to ask. "What are your choices?"

For the briefest moment, I debated not saying anything. After all, he hadn't told me what his deal was. But if I shared, maybe he would. Eventually.

"I need to find my mother, and I have a few mental images of where she might be, but nothing other than that."

"And your seer power won't help you?"

"I don't really have seer power. Not really." I'd always *thought* I was a seer, albeit a crappy one, but apparently that wasn't true at all. I was something else.

You are creation.

My mother's words echoed in my mind, and I frowned. Couldn't she have been more specific? I knew I had the power to force people to do my bidding, and I could sense danger. In some cases, I could even draw power from people. It was a magical hodgepodge, with no known species who could do such a strange assortment.

"Would a seer be able to help you?" he asked.

I turned to him. "A powerful one, maybe."

"Orinthia, the owner of this casino, is a seer."

"That's why you were here. Asking her about a cure."

He nodded.

Excitement flared. Maybe this was the answer. Fate's hand could have directed me toward Orinthia. "Let's ask her."

"She's downstairs on the casino floor. Come on."

I followed him to the elevator, stepping in to stand close to him. Closer than necessary, probably, but I wanted to be near him. It was a bad idea, but it was a compulsion I couldn't fight.

As the elevator zipped down to the bottom level, I took in the magnificent sight of the glittering city. Or I tried to, at least. Truthfully, all I could focus on was Drakon. I swore I could feel the heat of his shoulder across the scant inches that separated us, and his scent wrapped around me like an embrace.

Fates, I wanted to kiss him. An invisible force was pushing me toward him, and I didn't want to fight it.

By the time the doors opened, my breathing had quickened slightly, memories of our kiss driving it faster. Fortunately, the noise of the casino rushed in, breaking the spell.

I stepped out into the glittering space, taking in the

acrobats twirling from the ceiling by silken ribbons. All around, machines dinged and clanged, competing with the music and the murmur of gamblers at felt-covered tables.

"They're human," I murmured, surprised.

"Orinthia finds it easy to make a living off them."

"A very good living, I'm sure."

A waiter carrying a tray of complimentary drinks appeared in front of us, but Drakon waved him away. Free booze *and* gambling? This was Genevieve's idea of Paradise.

But how was she managing to play in a human casino? I searched the room for her but came up empty. It was too much to hope that she'd done the smart thing and gone home, but I didn't have time to worry about her right now. I'd deal with that problem when and if it came.

"This way." Drakon led me through the crowd, which parted to let him pass.

I followed, spotting a fantastically beautiful woman sitting on a throne on the far side of the room. A huge tiger lounged at her side.

Shifter.

No question.

The humans couldn't feel the magic emanating from the beast, but I could.

As for the seer—she was powerful as well. Her emerald eyes scanned the crowd with an uncanny knowledge, as if she could see right into their souls. When her gaze met mine, I shivered.

It felt like she could see into mine, as well.

As we approached her, the four guards who stood at her side moved to stand in front of her. She waved them off with a manicured hand and tilted her head as she stared at us.

"So you're the one that can help him." Her voice carried a hint of smoke as she inspected me.

"Me?" I glanced at Drakon's face, spotting the annoyance creasing his brow.

"Orinthia." His tone held a heavy dose of warning.

She shrugged. "What? *I* see no reason to hide anything."

"She's not the only one," Drakon said.

Orinthia hummed low, a sound that hinted at disagreement. "Let's have a drink."

She rose gracefully from the throne and sailed toward a table nearby. The white linen-covered surface was surrounded by a velvet rope, and we followed, taking a seat across from her. Within seconds, an assortment of cocktails was presented to us on a tray. She took a heavy crystal glass full of an amber liquid, and Drakon did the same. I chose a pink sparkly looking thing, but only took a tiny sip. It was so good—and I was so stressed—that I wanted to toss it back, but I resisted.

Orinthia met my gaze. "You need help."

"I do."

Orinthia gaze cut to Drakon. “Same again?”

He nodded. “I’ll make the transfer.”

They had to be talking about the cost of her services, and part of me wanted to argue. The other part was still annoyed, so I decided to just let him pay for me. Served him right for being such a secret-keeper.

Orinthia smiled and turned to me. “That settles it then. Give me your hand.”

I held out my hand, wincing when her fingertips brushed the back of it. Energy sparked from her, sharp and prickly.

She frowned, brow creasing. “There’s a lot going on inside you.”

“Any idea what I am?”

She shook her head. “Something weird, for sure.” She nodded toward Drakon. “His mate, definitely.”

“I know that. But I don’t know what I am, either.” It wasn’t the question I’d intended to ask, but it popped out anyway.

“You’re one of a kind, that’s for sure. But since I don’t know what, you should probably just focus on whatever you want my help with.”

I imagined my mother, trying to sink back into the vision she’d sent me.

Orinthia drew in a low breath. “I see her. You want to know where she is.”

“Yes.”

Orinthia’s magic swelled, and I waited, breath held.

"She's at Lakeland, in the Peak District."

"The estate that has been abandoned since that accident?" Drakon asked.

"The very same."

"Wait, what accident?" I asked.

They both looked at me, brows furrowed.

"It was big news about four or five years ago," Orinthia said. "No one knows what happened, but it was like a magical nuke went off at an ancient estate. Turned hundreds of acres into a wasteland."

I vaguely recalled hearing about it, though couldn't remember the details. "How did that happen?"

"No one knows." Orinthia grimaced. "But I wouldn't want to go there. They say the air itself is toxic."

Fantastic. "I'll find a way around it. Any more tips?"

"Be wary of your dreams. Danger lurks there."

"What do you mean? From my mother?"

"Not from her, no. Not in your dreams, at least. The threat comes from elsewhere, but I can't tell where."

I shivered. The vague warning just served to make me scared to go to sleep.

Her gaze flicked to Drakon. "As for tips....This one..."

I leaned forward, interested.

Drakon shook his head and stood. "We're done. Thank you for the help."

"Wait, I want to hear what she has to say about you," I said.

"No." His voice was hard enough to cut diamonds, and the seer shrugged.

"Sorry, chica. Can't share if he doesn't want me to."

Damn.

She looked at Drakon. "Don't forget to pay up."

"Of course." He stood, and I joined him.

Orinthia wiggled her fingers in a wave as Drakon and I turned to leave.

Genevieve.

I turned back. "Any chance you found a badger down here causing trouble?"

Orinthia's eyebrows rose. "Indeed, we did. She yours?"

"Yes. Is she okay?"

"We tried to take her into custody, but she bit two of my guards and disappeared."

I grimaced. "That's Genevieve, all right."

"Well, I liked her spunk. If we allowed magical beings, she'd be invited. As it is..." She shrugged. "It was weird, having a badger at the slots drinking a Manhattan she'd stolen from a grandmother from Cleveland."

"Yeah. Weird." I nodded my appreciation. "Thanks again."

"Any time. Especially when he pays." She grinned at Drakon.

He said nothing. Inclining his head at the seer, he led the way to the casino's exit. I followed, trailing behind in his wake as the crowd parted to let him pass.

The cool desert air was a welcome relief from the scent of booze, perfume, and sweat. It was still busy, but better than it had been inside. As cars zipped by on the street, I turned to Drakon. Before I could speak, he said, "I'm going with you to find your mother."

I felt my jaw slacken. "I didn't expect that. You've been avoiding me like I'm trying to sell tickets to your funeral."

The smallest and most reluctant smile tugged at his mouth, and I felt a brief surge of pleasure. I liked making this austere man smile.

"It's incredibly dangerous where you're going. I'm going to help."

He was right, of course. But the fact that he was willing to help was a surprise.

But then, was it really?

He'd stepped between me and danger every chance he'd gotten since we'd met. This was more of the same. He might be grumpy and terse, but he always had my back, never passing up an opportunity to protect me.

And honestly, I could use the help.

More than that, I wanted time with him to figure out what he wasn't telling me. The curse still haunted him, and I knew that there had to be something I could do to help.

I just needed time to figure it out.

This would buy me that time.

"All right. Let's go. I just need to pick up some things from my house first." Probably a lot of things, considering we were about to walk into a magical wasteland.

Here goes nothing.

3

Mac

By the time we arrived at Lakeland, it was mid-afternoon. Eve had needed a few hours to get us a potion that would help hold off the effects of the magically toxic air, but it had been worth the wait.

The whole place smelled like a combination of burning tires and dark magic, and I was sure I'd be unconscious already if I hadn't taken the potion.

Now that I stood at the edge of the clearing surrounding the manor house, anxiety was creeping across my skin.

"This is intense." I muttered, staring out at the pale yellow fog that crept along the dead grass. It burned my throat, and I tried to breathe as shallowly as possible.

In the distance, the mountains of the Peak District rose toward an ominous sky. Even though it was afternoon, the sky was dark as twilight. Streaks of black and gray intermingled with the heavy clouds. They roiled, threatening to pour on the huge manor house sitting on the edge of a dark, silent lake. Several outbuildings surrounded it, beautiful structures of wood and stone that looked like they'd been built hundreds of years ago.

I whistled low under my breath. "Whoever once lived here must have been loaded."

We'd tried to do a bit of research before coming here, but we'd learned nothing. The environmental effects of the disaster that had happened were well known in the magical community, but not the how or the why. It was as if they'd been wiped from the historical and mental record of anyone involved.

Curiosity still itched at me, though, fiercer than ever. How had my mother ended up here? Had she gotten on the bad side of whoever had once lived here?

But the place seemed empty.

"Where do you want to search first?" Drakon asked.

"The house. In my vision, she was in a stone-walled room. That could be a basement, I think."

"Let's go then."

I nodded and stepped out into the fog. Immediately, the air became thicker and more difficult to breathe. I coughed, pressing a hand to my chest.

"Let me try to teleport us." Drakon reached for my

arm and gripped it gently. I felt his magic tug on me, but the ether didn't suck us in as normal. He scowled. "Blocked."

I nodded. "No surprise. Let's run for it."

"Lead the way."

"No. You can out pace me any day. You go ahead."

"I'll be by your side." His voice was so gruff it sounded like it scraped over gravel.

I didn't argue. The smoke was making it hard to breathe, much less talk. Though Eve's potion was keeping us alive, it wasn't making this pleasant.

How the hell was my mother surviving here?

It had to be better in the house.

I kept that thought close as I sprinted toward the sprawling structure. My lungs burned and my muscles ached, the smoke seeming to seep inside me and light me on fire from within. We were only halfway there, and it already felt like I wasn't going to make it.

When the ground around us began to shift and crack, Drakon moved closer to me. Magic sparked in the air, and a low growl vibrated through the fog. A cold chill raced over me. All around, the earth began to split, deep crevasses opening in the grass.

From the cracks in the ground, creatures rose. Gaunt and skeletal, they appeared to be made of thorny tree roots twisted together. Four-legged, with stocky bodies and long faces, they were like nothing I'd ever seen before. Eerie green magic glowed from their eyes, and it was clear they weren't alive. Creatures of dark magic.

One by one, they clawed their way out of the earth until there were a dozen of them prowling toward us. The eerie yellow mist coiled around their feet.

Fear iced my skin, and I sprinted faster as the monsters tore themselves away from the roots that still bound them to the ground. Their growls grew louder, and I drew my sword from the ether.

The beasts charged, their eyes flaming.

Drakon intercepted the first one, grabbing it with his hands. He lifted it like it was nothing, tearing the head away from the body. The creature disappeared in a poof of dark smoke.

One of the monsters lunged for me, and I sliced out with my sword, decapitating it in a quick swipe. My blade cut through the neck like it was hacking through a collection of dried-up old tree limbs.

Dusty black magic exploded outward as it disappeared, and I held my breath as I sprinted past to avoid drawing any of it into my lungs. The next two creatures came more quickly, their massive forms charging across the dead grass.

Hellfire sparked on their breath, and I ducked the snapping bite of the first one, barely avoiding its thorny black teeth. As it sailed past me, I whirled around and slammed my blade through its neck, taking off the head.

The creature disappeared in a poof of dust as the second monster leapt for my throat.

I ducked low and stabbed my blade up through its chest. The sword cut through the thorny vines, but the beast didn't disappear like the others had. Still impaled on my blade, it snapped at me, fiery green eyes flashing.

Heart thundering, I jerked my arms to the side, trying to fling the beast away. It slid off my sword but came charging back. I barely managed to get my blade moving in time to slice its head off.

As the creature exploded into dust, another one took its place, moving so quickly that I didn't see it coming. It managed to sink its teeth into my arm. Icy pain flared from the spot, making my stomach pitch and my knees weaken.

Drakon appeared at my side. Yanking the creature off me, he tore it apart.

"There are too many," he said. "This isn't going to work."

He was right. The creatures kept rising out of the ground, and the misty air was making my lungs feel like I was on fire from the inside.

I searched the estate around us, looking for an escape route or a place to recoup our strength and come up with a plan.

We were still a long way from the main house, but there was something that looked like a stable between us and our target. I pointed to it. "The stable. We'll go there, bar the door, and come up with a plan."

"Follow me." Drakon sprinted across the ground, cutting a path through the creatures that charged us.

As the thorny beasts leapt up to try to take a bite out of his throat, he grabbed them and flung them aside. Occasionally, they managed to get their teeth into him, but he never flinched.

By the time we'd reached the stable, I felt like my legs were going to give out. Drakon heaved the heavy wooden door open, and I sprinted inside.

I heard the door slam behind me and turned to see Drakon bolting it behind us.

Panting, I went to my knees on the hard stone floor, clutching my chest as my lungs heaved and burned. "This place sucks."

"An understatement." Drakon stalked past me, inspecting the stable around us.

It wasn't dissimilar from the one we'd visited in Texas. Stalls lined either side of the main corridor in which I knelt, but the air echoed with emptiness and neglect. Holes in the roof allowed a small amount of light to stream through. Beams of it glittered on the dust motes and illuminated the ancient space.

Growls sounded from outside as the beasts threw themselves at the door.

"They're not going anywhere," Drakon said.

He was right. And I doubted I'd be lucky enough to

find my mother in this stable. I could feel her, though, I was sure of it. This estate was definitely the right place to look, and I'd give the stable a good search just to be sure.

I staggered to my feet and approached Drakon, inspecting the punctures and tears to his skin. He'd been bitten over a dozen times, and the wounds bled sluggishly.

My heart twisted, and I raised a hand, nearly pressing it to his chest. I drew back at the last moment. The last thing he needed was for me to touch him. "You're hurt."

"I'm fine." His gaze lingered on mine, flickering with something I couldn't quite put my finger on. Almost like he wanted to look away but couldn't make himself.

"Let me get you a healing potion." I reached for the bag that Eve had given me to store in the ether, but he shook his head.

"I'm going to get more injured than this. Let's save it." He stalked around me, heading down the corridor. "We need to find a way out of here. Or a way to take out a lot of those creatures at once."

"Can't argue with that." I left the bag in the ether and turned to follow him.

As I walked down the long, dark passage, an image of a black horse flashed into my mind.

A stallion, standing in a stall just like the ones to my left and right.

Frowning, I searched the area around me, looking for something familiar. But the feeling had passed.

"Are you all right?" Drakon's voice snapped me to attention, and I looked over to find him staring at me with concern on his face.

"Yeah, fine."

"All right. But you've been standing in that spot for a good three minutes."

"Three minutes?" Surprise flashed through me. "Felt like seconds."

Concern creased his brow. "What's going on?"

I shivered, then shook off the feeling. "Nothing. It's fine. Let's keep looking."

The stables were empty, as I'd expected, and I didn't get any more strange visions. Though we didn't find a secret passageway into a dungeon holding my mother, we did find a few gallons of linseed oil in one of the stock rooms.

I eyed it, then turned to Drakon. "What do you think of luring them in here, then lighting them up?"

Normally, the idea would make me cringe. I could never do that to any living creature, no matter how badly it wanted to kill me. But these creatures weren't living. They were made of dark magic and thorny roots—unfeeling and unthinking, driven to destroy by the spell that had created this horrific magical wasteland.

"I like how you think." He picked up two of the large containers, and I joined him, collecting two of my own.

Together, we doused the piles of hay and the dry wooden stall doors with the oil. As we worked, the door at the far end of the stable rattled from the attacks of the creatures. Their growls carried through as they tried to beat it down.

Finally, we'd poured out every container of oil. This place would go up like a bonfire on Guy Fawkes' Day. If there was someone in the manor house, they would see us for sure. I didn't see how we had any alternative, though.

I tossed aside the last can and looked at Drakon. "Are you thinking we let them in that door"—I pointed to the one that they pounded upon, then turned around and pointed to the one at the other end of the long corridor—"and then we run out that door?"

"Exactly." He nodded to the far door. "You go over there. Then I'll let them in and join you. We'll light it up, and then I'll run around the outside of the barn and shut this door behind them."

He was a *hell* of a lot faster than me, but even that could be a stretch. I shook my head. "Our best bet is for you to wait at the far door, and I'll let them in and lead them into the barn. You use that time to sneak around the outside and shut the door behind them."

He frowned. "Too dangerous."

"It's too dangerous to fail at this. You know my way is best, and I'll be fast enough."

His scowl didn't disappear, but he nodded. "Fine."

I gripped the matches I'd found as I watched him stride to the far end of the barn. At least it stood silent and still, indicating that the dark magic beasts were too stupid to try to find another entry. They didn't have brains, merely instincts driven by the spell that had created them.

When Drakon reached the far door, I nodded at him, then went to the door that rattled from the repeated blows of the monsters who stalked us.

I drew a potion bomb from the bag that Eve had packed for me, making sure to choose one that would ignite the oil. Prepared, I pulled open the door to the barn. The creatures lunged inside as I spun around and began to run. I'd never sprinted so fast in my life.

On the far end of the barn, Drakon disappeared out the door.

As the beasts nipped at my heels, I sprinted after him. When I was nearly there, I hurled the potion bomb over my shoulder. Though I didn't turn to look, I heard it explode. Heat flared against my back as the oil ignited. The beasts made no noise, but I couldn't hear as many footsteps following me.

I reached the far door and slipped through. The yellow fog clogged my lungs as I spun around to see the beasts charging the door, flames filling the barn around them. I slammed the doors shut.

It rattled as the creatures threw themselves against it, but I didn't stick around. There were no monsters out here—not on this side of the barn, at least—but I needed to find Drakon.

Lungs burning, I ran around the side of the barn, finding him on the opposite side, bolting the barn door.

"They all went in," he said.

"Good." Smoke had begun to waft from the roof, and I stared up at it, trying not to feel guilty.

"They feel nothing," Drakon said. "They might be shaped like animals, but they are made of tree roots and magic. They have no consciousness."

"How could you tell that was what I was thinking?"

"You're a good person."

I wasn't sure about that, but now wasn't the time to argue. "Let's go. I can't stand out here a minute longer."

The barn hadn't had as much of the horrible fog inside of it, and I was hopeful the house would be the same.

Together, we set off across the grass, sprinting toward the house. It loomed in the distance, fabulous and terrifying all at once. I didn't have an eye for architecture, but the massive stone structure looked like it had been built hundreds of years ago. The windows gleamed dully beneath the faint light of the afternoon, and a dozen chimneys rose silently toward the clouds.

Still, the place seemed to echo with misery, as if it had been imbued into the stones.

Together, we sprinted toward the wide stone stairs in front of the main door.

So close.

We were almost there.

Behind us, the barn was alight. A quick glance back showed the biggest fire I'd ever seen, black smoke curling toward the sky as the yellow flames licked at the wood.

Most importantly, none of the dark magic creatures were running toward us.

I turned back to the house, heart hopeful. We were going to make it.

The house beckoned, the double doors closed but welcoming. Huge stairs led up to them, surrounded on either side by pillars that were covered in dead rose vines. They were as thorny and thick as the dead roots that had created the monsters.

We reached the stairs and I leapt up onto them. Drakon followed, but as he took his second step onto the stair, one of the thick old rose vines tore away from the pillar to his left.

I caught sight of it out of the corner of my eye and turned. It all happened so fast.

One moment, Drakon was racing up the stairs. The next, the rose vine had lashed out and pierced him straight through the chest.

He stopped abruptly, shock widening his eyes as the vine lifted him up in the air.

Horror turned my limbs to ice. I reached for him. "No!"

Blood seeped from the corner of his mouth as he reached for the vine that plunged into his chest, but he didn't have the traction required to pull it free.

I drew my sword and lunged, slicing through the vine. He crashed to the ground, and the vines lashed out to attack him once more.

"No!" I hacked at them with my blade, cutting through them as they reached for him. "Stop!"

Oddly, they seemed to listen. The vines fell silent and dead, and I reached for Drakon, helping him to his feet. He staggered upright, the vine still punching through his chest. His normally brilliant blue eyes were dull, and his breathing was shallow.

"Come on." I dragged him toward the door, which opened easily, thank fates.

The vines lay silent as we left them, but I didn't take the time to wonder. My mind was entirely on Drakon. The wound in his chest was horrific, and the vine was still inside him.

I didn't know who or what we'd find in this house, but it had to be better than what was outside.

As soon as we stepped over the threshold, he went to his knees on the marble. The air was better in here, but he looked worse, the wound quickly sapping his strength.

I spun toward him, barely seeing the house through my fear. It felt empty, and I hoped that meant it bought us a few safe moments.

"Drakon." I went to my knees in front of him as he sat back on his heels, propping himself up with one arm. He was barely able to support his own weight.

With shaking hands, I drew a healing potion from Eve's bag. It was the strongest one she'd given me, and I prayed it would work.

"I need to take the vine out."

"Just do it. I'll be fine." His eyes had turned nearly black, and he leaned over farther. He couldn't lie on the floor—the damned vine was protruding from his back —and he'd only do himself more damage.

My stomach turned at the idea of yanking the vine out, but it had to be done if he was going to heal. I'd cut it off from the front, so I moved behind him and started to count to three.

On two, I yanked the vine free.

A low, pained groan escaped him as he collapsed onto his back.

"Drink this." I lifted him up, terrified at how limp his muscles were, and poured the potion down his throat.

He swallowed, but his dark eyes just turned cloudier and more vacant. His skin was so pale that he could have been a ghost.

"Come on, Drakon." Fear echoed in my voice. "Come on."

The damage to his chest was terrifying. Hell, I could see straight through to the floor below. He was supposed to be immortal, but the curse had sapped so much of his strength that I didn't think he was anymore.

In fact, I could feel his pain and weakness as if it were my own. Wherever I touched him, it flowed straight into me, racing through my veins and muscles.

Gasping, I knelt over him, barely able to keep myself upright. Our connection was binding us in a way I'd never experienced, making it feel like we were the same person.

When his eyes fluttered closed and his body went slack, horror hollowed my insides. I could *feel* his life force drifting from him.

Drakon was dying.

4

Mac

I stared down at Drakon's slack form, fear turning my body to ice.

Dying.

He couldn't be dying.

He was supposed to be immortal.

And yet, right now... he wasn't.

The curse.

Shaking, I shoved the thought away. It didn't matter why, just that it *was*. And I needed to do something about it.

My blood.

If Eve's healing potion wasn't working, my blood might. It had worked before. And right now, I didn't care if there would be consequences from sharing my blood with him.

I had to do everything I could. Terror twisted my heart. The idea of losing him was more than I could bear.

My arms trembled as I lifted his head into my lap and raised a wrist to his mouth. He lay slack and unmoving.

Damn it.

Quickly, I used my sword to make a small cut at my wrist. Pain flared and blood welled. Drakon shifted. He might be unconscious, but his instincts weren't.

As I pressed the bleeding wound to his lips, a low rumble escaped his chest. He sank his fangs into my skin, and pleasure shot through me.

"Come on, drink," I whispered.

As he drew on my wrist, I felt it tug deep inside me, sending waves of pleasure through my core. I ignored them, focusing on healing Drakon. I could feel it reflected inside myself. The connection that bound us, and I felt him healing. As I watched, the wound in his chest began to close.

Hope flared.

"Come on, open your eyes," I said, adjusting my wrist so that he could keep drinking. It was beginning to make me feel a bit woozy, but the positive reinforcement of watching him heal kept me in place.

When he finally opened his eyes, my heart nearly exploded with relief.

"You're okay." I wanted to hug him close but didn't dare. Instead, I withdrew my wrist and pressed it against my shirt to stop the bleeding.

His brow creased as he raised a hand to his lips and wiped away the blood staining them "You fed me your blood."

"Of course. You were dying."

"Damn it, you shouldn't have done that."

I frowned and leaned back on my heels, separating from him as he sat up.

"What's wrong?" I asked. "You look pissed, and I just saved your life."

"I'm immortal. I didn't need you to save me."

"Yes, you did. I could feel the life seeping from you. The curse has weakened you."

His eyes flickered with confusion, then acknowledgment. Or maybe it was something else.

"Tell me what's going on with you," I demanded.

He surged to his feet, as strong as he'd ever been, but way more pissed. He ignored my question, of course. "You should have asked."

"Should have asked your unconscious body?"

His jaw tightened as if he recognized how ridiculous that sounded but didn't want to admit it. "I don't want your blood."

"Sure you don't."

His jaw tightened with anger, and I could feel that there was something left unsaid between us. Maybe it was my magic, maybe instinct, but there was something going on. Something connected to my blood.

I tilted my head. "You've drunk from thousands of people in your immortal life. What is it about *my* blood that's so repugnant to you?"

"It's not repugnant."

"Then what is it?"

"I just don't want it."

"*That's* what's weird, though. It's just blood."

His gaze flashed. "You have no idea what you're talking about."

"Maybe not. But I want you to explain it to me. Something is definitely up with you, and I want to know what."

"Not everything is your business, Mac. Don't do that again."

I stood, annoyed by what a dick he was being. I didn't need him to be on his knees with gratitude, but this was too much. "Fine, whatever."

He rose and turned to inspect the foyer in which we stood. I'd barely looked at it before, but a quick glance highlighted the most relevant features—soaring ceiling, huge staircase, dusty windows. It reeked of old money and power, and definitely a butt load of misery.

"There's no one here," I said. "Can you feel how empty it is?"

He nodded. "But what about your mother? Can you feel her?"

I closed my eyes and drew in a deep breath, focusing on the feeling I'd gotten during the dream. It was like we were connected with our minds, and I *could* actually feel her.

"She's near. I'm pretty sure my vision showed her in a cell underground, so maybe that's why I don't feel any living people."

"But there are no guards inside the house."

"Not that I can feel. We could always be surprised, though." Still, worry tugged at me.

"Let's start looking. Bottom floor first?"

"Yes." How long had she been here? Could she possibly still be alive?

Yes. I'd seen her in my visions. Felt her. She was here.

My heart raced as we began to search, anxiety driving me forward. I hadn't even known she'd existed last week, and now I was desperate to find her.

She had answers.

And she was...family. I didn't know if I loved her. Didn't know if I could trust her. She definitely wasn't the family I'd thought I'd had—that had been a fake memory implanted by persons unknown—but she was family all the same.

It would have been faster to split up to search for her, but I didn't want to. Danger lurked around every corner, and we'd need to be together to survive this place.

Drakon stuck close by my side as I headed toward the wide hallway to the left. His gaze kept scanning the premises and back to me, as though checking to make sure that I was still okay.

I wasn't, but I also wasn't about to keel over. Given the circumstances, that was a win.

The house was eerily silent as we walked down the wide hallway. A crimson rug ran down the middle of the wooden floor, a thick layer of dust making it appear dull. Faint, late-evening sunset gleamed through the window at the end, providing just enough light to illuminate the paintings on the wall.

They were all portraits, the eyes of the people in the frames following us as we walked. A shiver raced down my spine.

When we came to the first door, I followed Drakon inside a sitting room filled with fussy furniture and a tiny, ancient piano-like instrument. Something about it made the hair raise on the back of my neck, and I shivered.

"Do you feel that?" I asked.

"Feel what?"

Guess not. "Just something weird."

Fortunately, it didn't take long to search. There were no secret doors or hollow places in the floor that might lead to a dungeon, so we kept going, searching every room off the hallway. It wasn't until we reached the library that the strangest feeling of awareness came over me.

I stopped dead in the doorway, staring inside.

"Are you all right?" Drakon asked.

"Yeah." *Not really.* I drew in a shuddery breath as I inspected the space. It was also oddly familiar, but even more so.

"You're not." He gripped my bicep with a comforting hand, and I leaned into him.

I shouldn't. Turning to him for comfort was no doubt a bad idea. But I couldn't help it. There was just something about him. About our connection.

I'm falling for him.

Hell, I probably already had.

I drew strength from him, then stepped forward and entered the room. As if in a trance, I went to the shelf and picked up one of the books. As I opened it, the pages within crumbled to dust.

Gasping, I nearly dropped it. "That's weird."

Drakon picked up a different one, and the same thing happened. "Perhaps whatever magic cursed this place has destroyed the books."

"What a weird spell." I slipped the hollow book back on the shelf. As I did so, a vision flashed in my mind—me, as a child, doing something very similar.

Oh shit.

Awareness crashed into me. "I think this was my house when I was young."

Genevieve appeared at my side, hugging my leg as if she could sense that I was rattled.

"Do you remember this room?" Drakon asked.

"Kind of. It's more a feeling of knowing." I spun around to look at it, trying to bring forth more memories. Nothing came, and frustration tightened my chest, making it harder to breathe. "Damn it, I just want to remember."

"You will." Though he was clearly trying to make his voice sound comforting, it wasn't quite working. He was as skeptical as I was.

"Whoever erased my memory did a damned good job." Frustration tightened my lungs, turning to something like panic.

Genevieve hugged my calf harder. *You clearly came from money. Maybe you were a horrible snob and don't want to remember.*

A small laugh escaped me, making me feel a bit better. I bent down and ruffled her head. "Yeah."

We both knew it was bullshit, but it was easier to pretend than to stare headlong into the mystery haunting me. Anyway, I needed to focus if I wanted to solve it.

Instead of searching through more of the library, I decided to call on my new magic. Maybe that could help me.

I closed my eyes and focused on my mother, trying to draw up the connection. Nothing happened. I tried harder.

Still nothing.

Damn it.

Frustration surged anew. "Why the hell can't I control my new magic? What do I have to do to get it to work?"

The question was rhetorical, and from their silence, my companions could clearly tell. Genevieve just hugged my leg harder, while Drakon said nothing.

"It's fine. Let's keep going." I started forward, determined to keep moving.

Genevieve scampered away. *I'll search, too.*

"Thank you."

Together, the three of us moved through the house. I looked at everything with new eyes, trying to remember something about my life here. *Anything.*

I didn't, but at least I didn't have another panic attack. As the sun set, we searched every room on the bottom floor of the house. I looked for clues about my past as well as for my mother but found neither.

By the time we made it to the upper floor, I felt like I'd been searching for ten years. The halls stretched out on either side of us, dotted with rooms that beckoned for us to explore.

The idea exhausted me.

"We should take a break," Drakon said.

I leaned against the wall and thumped my head back. "I doubt she's on this floor anyway. The cell she's in is clearly a stone-walled basement location."

I walked to one of the windows and looked out. Full dark had fallen, yet the disgusting yellow mist still glowed under the light of the moon. It was thicker now, and higher. Would Eve's protective potion even work against it in these circumstances?

Maybe. Maybe not.

But I could feel the danger outside, pressing in on the windows. There was still intense magic out there, and in the dark, it'd be even harder to see it coming at us.

"We should get some rest," Drakon said. "We'll need to finish in the morning when it's safer."

I turned to look at him, noting that there were no shadows under his eyes or sag to his shoulders. He had plenty of energy. When he'd said *we,* he'd been talking about me.

And he was right. I just needed a damned break from this. The longer I went without my memory of my past, the more I considered the possibility that I didn't *want* to remember. Part of me hated the mystery, part of me wondered if I were better off not knowing.

It's dinnertime, Genevieve said. *I'll bring you a picnic.*

I looked down at her. "Thanks, pal."

She nodded and disappeared.

I looked at Drakon. "Let's find a place to eat."

We located a sitting room a short way down the hall, and Drakon lit a fire. The warmth billowed out, and I pulled an armchair closer, collapsing into it. Every muscle ached from exhaustion, and I stared into the flames.

Drakon joined me, and Genevieve appeared shortly after. She had a grocery sack full of random things from the Shadow Guild kitchen, and she dumped it out on the low table in front of us.

It was a motley assortment, trending more toward sugar than anything else, but there was enough to make ham sandwiches.

"Thanks, pal."

Together, Drakon and I made our dinner in silence. Genevieve stuck mostly to the sweets, then disappeared with a wave.

When I finished eating, I stared into the flickering flames. "I thought I'd find clues about my past here."

"You remember nothing?"

"Nothing valuable. Just brief flashes." I looked at him.

The firelight flickered over his face, casting him in golden glows and shadows that highlighted his mystery and beauty. I couldn't believe someone could look like him—both powerful and gorgeous at the same time.

"Do you remember your childhood?" I asked.

"Never had one. I was created, not born."

"Right. Created of magic and blood."

He nodded.

"By whom?"

"I don't know." He frowned into the flame.

"Does that bother you?"

He shrugged. "Maybe once, so long ago that I don't recall. Now, it's difficult to be bothered by something that happened so many years ago."

A thousand years.

It really was impossibly long. What must it have been like to live so long?

Lonely.

And did he really not care who had made him? From the tense set to his jaw and the shadows in his eyes, that had been a lie. Drakon wasn't used to confiding in others. Of course not, after so long alone. The fact that he told me anything at all was surprising.

"Do you mind being immortal?" I asked.

"Mind?" He frowned, brow creasing, as if he'd never considered it before. "Of course not. I love it."

"Really? Seems like it would be lonely to me."

Drakon

I love it.

The words I'd just said echoed in my head. Did I really love it?

Once, yes.

Now?

Perhaps.

But sitting across from her, enjoying a simple meal by the fire, was the best thing I'd experienced in centuries. Maybe ever.

When she was gone, I'd no longer have this.

Hell, I wouldn't be able to have it now if I didn't find a solution to the curse that was turning me to granite.

So, no, immortality wasn't quite working for me anymore. Not after meeting her. Just the idea of being parted from her made something shrivel up inside me. I'd rather be dead.

A soft, bitter laugh escaped me.

I might be *dead soon.*

"What is it?" she asked.

"Nothing."

"It's something. Tell me."

Doing that would just put more pressure on her, so I said nothing.

Not to be deterred, Mac reached out and gripped my arm. The gesture was clearly meant to be comforting, and I couldn't help but lean into the warmth of her touch.

She gasped and yanked her hand back.

A crack appeared in the place where I might have

had a heart, and I looked at her. I should expect her rejection, but I still didn't like it.

"Drakon." Worry echoed in her voice.

I looked at her, and she slowly reached a hand toward me to grip my shoulder. When she made contact, pain flashed in her eyes.

"What's wrong? Are you all right?"

She nodded, her mouth tight. "I don't know. Sometimes, I can feel what you feel. Like we're connected."

"What do you mean?"

She gripped my arm harder, flinching. "It doesn't happen all the time, but occasionally, I feel what it's like to turn to granite. It hurts."

"It's fine. I'm working on it."

She squinted at me, her magic flaring in the air. "It's not fine. And you're not working on it."

"I've no idea what you mean."

She gasped, yanking her hand back again. "It's something about my blood. I can feel it—that's what heals you."

I looked toward the flames, knowing that she'd be able to read the lie in my words as soon as they left my mouth.

"Why won't you drink my blood if it will heal you?" she demanded.

"It doesn't heal me. It just keeps me from becoming entrapped in granite."

"What's the damned difference?" Frustration surged in her voice.

"It's not just one dose." My heart thundered as I turned to her, hopelessness and anger pounding hard. "It's every day of your life."

"Shit." She blinked, staring at me. "Really?"

"Really." And her response was exactly what I'd expected. It was entirely reasonable. Who wouldn't reject the idea?

"It's fine." She gripped my arm tighter. "I don't mind."

"You don't mind?" I frowned at her. "Are you mad?"

"If it helped you, it'd be worth it."

"I can't do that to you. Five years ago, you locked me away to avoid this fate. You might have forgotten your memory, but its only reasonable to assume you knew this would be your life if you met me. You wanted to stop it."

"We don't know that." But something flashed in her eyes—something like surprise or recognition. Both.

I couldn't read it for sure.

"Let me decide," she said.

"No." I stood. This conversation was over. "We should get some sleep."

She scowled at me as she stood but said nothing more about the issue. I could see the thoughts turning behind her eyes, though. This wasn't over.

I left the room to find a bedroom, waiting briefly to

make sure she followed. She did, and I continued down the hall. So far, the house seemed safer than the grounds outside, but we had no idea how long that would last. I didn't want her left alone while we were here.

Which meant sleeping would prove to be an issue.

Fortunately, I found a room on the top floor that contained a bed and a long couch. I nodded toward the bed, which was draped in rich crimson velvet. "For you."

"And what about you?"

I tilted my head toward the couch. "That will do."

"It's too short for you."

"It'll be fine."

She huffed a small sigh, then went to the bed and yanked the velvet coverlet away. A small plume of dust rose into the air as she dropped it to the ground at the foot of the bed.

I made a point not to look at her as she sat on the side of the bed and took off her boots. I could hear clothing rustling, though, and it took everything I had not to imagine her removing it and revealing the smooth skin beneath.

Desire tightened within me, and I threw myself on the couch.

She was not for me.

No matter how much I might want her.

No matter what fate said.

The covers of the bed shifted, and I judged it safe to

look. I turned. She was in the bed, the sheets pulled up to her chin and a pile of her clothing on the floor beside her. At best, she was only in her undergarments.

The sight hit me like a bolt of lightning, and I turned my face back up to the ceiling and tried to fall asleep. My preternaturally good hearing was a curse, however, and I could hear her every movement against the sheets, her every breath.

Memories flashed in my mind—every touch we'd shared, every kiss. They haunted me as I tried to find sleep, tightening everything inside me.

It was going to be a long night.

5

Mac

Dreams sent me back to the past—back to the moment I first saw Drakon. He was walking into my pub once more, angry as hell and out for blood.

Adrenaline raced through my veins, just like it had that night. I could still feel the connection between us, the intensity of the bond that I didn't yet understand.

Mates.

Somehow, fate had chosen us to be perfect for one another.

I'd thought fate was wrong.

But as the dream played in my mind, racing forward through every moment that we'd spent together, it was impossible to believe that fate was so misguided.

My mind replayed every interaction as if I were watching a movie, skipping from moment to moment as he protected me. As we grew closer. I watched as we fought together and laughed and kissed.

From this angle, it was impossible not to fall for him. It didn't matter how much my conscious mind resisted the idea—the rest of me knew that he was perfect.

Damaged, yes. And difficult.

But perfect for me.

And all I had to do was give him a bit of my blood every day to keep him alive.

That wasn't so difficult, even though the idea was terrifying.

The act would bond us in a way that was breakable only by death. Even then, our connection would remain.

The idea sent another image into my mind—Drakon, turned entirely to stone, his soul trapped in granite.

The memory made my stomach pitch and my heart pound. Horror opened a giant chasm within my chest, loss threatening to overwhelm me. To know that he was trapped within the rock made every inch of my body and every bit of my soul wail with grief.

He was so close, and yet so far away. This loss was worse than death.

I choked on the pain, unable to escape it.

Was this a vision of the future? Or just a dream of what I feared?

Would this come true?

I couldn't bear the thought. It made me want to wail, to rage against fate and the impossible situation it had put us in. I wanted to destroy things, to take out my grief and rage and loss on something else.

The feeling was nearly overwhelming, making my mind go dark with loss and panic. I felt like I was drowning, losing myself in grief and rage.

It weakened me, and I felt my mind faltering. My defenses lowered, and something else entered my dreams.

Ludovic.

I could feel his presence like he was there. Suddenly, I wasn't alone anymore. I wasn't even in a true dream state.

Magic pulled at me, the unmistakable pull of the ether. It wrapped around my limbs and tried to tear me from my dream.

Somehow, Ludovic had gotten ahold of me. His icy grip was strong on my arms as he tried to steal me away. This had become real. He was here, trying to kidnap me once more.

I screamed, trying to pull myself free. I fought his grip with everything I had, trying to break away from the magic that wrapped around me and threatened to take me somewhere terrible. Panic flared, and my heart raced.

"Mac! Mac!"

The voice echoed in the chaos of my mind, a light in the darkness. I clung to it, trying to find my way out.

"I'm here, Mac. You're not alone."

Gasping, I tried to follow the voice. It was the only way out of this abyss of fear and pain. The only way to get away from Ludovic.

Drakon.

He was alive, and he was calling to me.

He was more real than Ludovic. More real than the terrible vision that foretold his death—I just had to escape the trap of my mind. The trap that Ludovic had set.

As my senses returned, I could feel the warmth of his arms around me. The strength of his chest beneath my cheek. He kept talking— reassuring words that became my lifeline.

He's here.

The words became my mantra, and I repeated them to myself as I surfaced from the fog of nightmares.

When my vision returned and consciousnesses crashed over me, I gasped.

Drakon held me in his arms, strength and warmth surrounding me. His beautiful face was creased with lines of worry, his blue eyes dark with concern.

I looked up at him, my heart thundering as I took in the flash of his eyes and the warmth of his skin.

Alive.

Relief rushed through me.

"You were having a nightmare." Worry roughened his tone. "But I felt another presence."

"Ludovic." I gasped, clinging to him.

"What do you mean?"

"He was in my dream somehow. A spell linking him to me. Like how my mother can enter my mind, but even worse. I think he was trying to kidnap me."

"When I saw you, your form was flickering. As if you were about to disappear."

Fear iced down my spine. Ludovic really was trying to kidnap me through my dreams. Fates, whatever magic made that possible was terrifying.

"You're safe now." Drakon held me tightly, and I let him, reveling in the feeling of protection.

"You're pale as a ghost."

That wasn't a surprise. I felt as ephemeral as one, too. As if I would blow away on a strong wind, my atoms dispersed into the universe.

It felt like he anchored me to the world.

"What were you dreaming?" he asked.

I didn't want to let go of him, but the longer I clung to his strength, the weirder it was going to get.

I was choosing to hold onto him for comfort, and I was going to have to acknowledge that eventually. Or let go.

I didn't want to let go of him.

I never wanted to let go.

"Will you just lie here with me?" The words escaped

before I could think about them, but as soon as I heard them, I realized how badly I wanted that. Just to lie with him, wrapped in his strength.

"Yes." His voice scraped over gravel on the way out of his throat.

I shifted the sheets so he could slip under them. He was still fully dressed, but I didn't care. It was for the best, in fact.

As he wrapped his arms around me, my heartbeat settled down. His strength imbued me with calm, and I sighed contentedly.

"This is nice." The words slipped out, and I regretted them immediately.

It almost felt like I should pretend this wasn't happening. It was one thing to lose my mind and kiss him. It was another to be fully conscious of my actions and ask him to snuggle with me because I was scared.

That was some real life, official relationship stuff right there.

And he hadn't responded to my ridiculous *this is nice.*

Had I made it weird?

I'd made it weird.

Shit.

"It is." His words rushed over me like a balm.

I said no more—just focused on his warmth and strength and the feeling of one-thousand-percent rightness that flowed through me.

I shouldn't care for him.

But how could I not?

His life had been so long and hard and lonely, and yet he was still fundamentally good. Despite all the dark things he'd done—he was the first vampire, after all, I couldn't expect a spotless record—his soul wasn't irrevocably tarnished. He tried to be better.

The idea of falling asleep terrified me, but exhaustion finally won out. I drifted off, wrapped in a feeling of warmth and comfort that I wanted to take with me for the rest of my life.

If I dreamed, I didn't remember it. Ludovic didn't return. When I woke, it was to cool sheets and no Drakon.

There was a massively heavy weight on my chest, however. Upon opening my eyes, I spotted a furry black and white face only a foot from my own.

Genevieve sat on my chest, her keen black eyes riveted to me.

You snore.

"I do not."

Denial doesn't look good on you.

I grumbled and shoved her off me. She tumbled to the soft bed and grunted. *That's the thanks I get for bringing you breakfast?*

I looked at a battered white bag next to me. "Rubbish bin croissants?"

They put them in a plastic bag before they put them in

the bin, so they're perfectly good. The bakery shouldn't throw them out after only one day. So wasteful!

"Not when you're around."

True. I'm an environmentalist, not a thief. We can't have the landfills getting overfilled with pastry. It would be a catastrophe.

"Utter chaos." I picked up the bag and removed a stale croissant. Hunger gnawed at my stomach, and I figured beggars couldn't be choosers. And Genevieve was picky, even though she found her breakfast in the bins. She'd only take them if they were clean. "Where's Drakon?"

He was searching the other rooms when I arrived.

As if I'd summoned him, he appeared in the doorway. Even though he'd slept in his clothes, they somehow still managed to look perfect on him.

"Are you all right?" he asked.

"No more nightmares." Ludovic had stayed away, but the memory of Drakon's death still haunted me.

No, not his death.

Worse than death.

Death would take one to an afterlife—not a bad situation, for most. But having your soul entombed in granite?

That would be hell.

I sat up, about to climb out of bed, and remembered that I was only in my bra and panties.

Had we really slept like this last night? I'd barely

been dressed. Heat flushed to my cheeks, and Drakon turned around.

As quickly as I could, I threw on my old clothes and tugged on my shoes. When I was done, I said, "Genevieve brought breakfast."

She grabbed the bag and toddled over to him, giving him her best toothy grin.

"Thank you." He took it but didn't eat. "I've searched the rest of the upstairs and didn't find anything. Do you want to look?"

"Let me try my magic." I'd assumed she was in the house, but it seemed I was wrong about that. Perhaps I could get us closer if I tried working smarter instead of harder.

The window called to me, and I walked toward it. The day was cloudy and gray, the sun hidden behind a thick wall of fog. From there, I could see the skeleton of the charred barn and a bit of the lake that I hadn't recalled until this moment.

"Still looks haunted." I rested my hand on the window frame and closed my eyes. Since I still didn't know what kind of supernatural I was, I'd have to use instinct. My magic called to me quite clearly, making it easier than I'd expected. It was as if parts of my mind were unlocking.

Because I was there?

Because I was starting to remember my past?

Probably a bit of both.

The strange magic of my mind thrummed through me, lighting up all my nerve endings with a tingling sense of awareness. Serenity filled me, making me feel like I was one with everything around me. My atoms blended with the ones in the air, and I felt infinite.

"The lake." It filled my mind, clear as day. "She's near the lake."

"Is there a building there? Some place for the dungeon you saw in your vision?"

"An...island." A small island covered in trees formed slowly in my mind. "There's something there. An ancient, sacred place."

"Let's go."

I opened my eyes. "I can't believe that worked."

"I can. Do you think your mother will have answers about what you are?"

"That's what I'm hoping."

Together, we left the bedroom and made our way to the first floor. The house was still eerily silent, every inch of it covered in a faint dust that spoke of years of neglect.

"What the hell happened here, exactly?" I asked.

"I don't know any more than what we discussed at the casino. An explosion of some kind—magical, definitely. But who did it.... No idea."

"My parents clearly pissed someone off."

He opened the door and stared out at the sickly fog that rolled over the ground. "Someone powerful."

"No kidding." I coughed as the fog rolled into the house. Eve's potion would work for another twenty-four hours, but after that, we'd have to leave. "Let's be quick."

"Don't like this place?"

"Even without the fog, I think I'd hate it." I turned to look back into the massive entry hall. "Who would want to grow up here? It's like a mausoleum."

"Couldn't say."

"Right. Of course." He *hadn't* grown up. He'd been created, fully formed as an adult. That was...tragic, in a way. Not to have a childhood.

But then again, my childhood might have sucked royally. I didn't remember it, but this place was kind of a nightmare. Even without the miserable fog and murderous beasts, it felt like it had been a dark and dreary home. It would have been a shitty place to have a childhood if I'd had one at all.

Maybe Drakon and I were kindred spirits in a sense, then.

"Ready?" he asked.

I nodded, realizing that my mind had drifted away for a moment. He did that to me—stole my senses. Stole my *sense.* Caring for him was crazy. Dangerous. And yet, I couldn't help myself.

"Yeah. Let's go."

We set off across the grass, moving swiftly toward the lake. Every sense was on high alert as I looked out for attack. Danger filled the air, prickling against my skin. The mist that rolled along the ground was thick and yellow. It burned my lungs, and I did my best to breathe shallowly.

Fortunately, none of the dark magic monsters appeared. It seemed we'd destroyed them all, thank fates. The morning sun was weak as we approached the lake, shedding barely enough light to cut through the fog. It felt like the entire place was shrouded in constant shadows, as if it couldn't shake off a dark past.

The longer I spent there, the more certain I became that it hadn't been a happy home.

Damn it, I needed to stop being so negative.

We were here to find my mother. It might all work out wonderfully.

Sure.

Finally, we reached the lake. The water gleamed like a dark mirror, hinting at secrets beneath the surface. It had the haunted feeling of a place that was inhabited by mermaids who would try to drag you to your death.

A small island sat in the middle of the lake with tall, skeletal trees reaching toward the sky. I pointed to it. "She's there."

"Do you remember anything about it?"

Images flashed in my mind—a boat and long afternoons on the island. The trees had been alive then, and I'd loved that place. "A bit. But no helpful details. Except..."

I looked to the right, expecting to see a boathouse.

When I did, I smiled. "Looks like my memory is returning a bit. I think we'll find a rowboat in there."

"Let's go." He set off along the pebbly shore.

I followed, my gaze moving between the island and the boathouse. No more memories returned, but that didn't stop me from trying to dredge them up.

The boathouse was a ramshackle old building that looked like it had been standing since the dawn of time. We found an ancient rowboat inside, and Drakon dragged it to the waterline. Small waves lapped at the bow, and he nodded to it. "Get in and I'll push you out."

"Thanks." I wasn't keen on getting my boots wet, so I took him up on the offer and climbed into the small boat.

I took the seat in the bow, and he pushed the vessel out into the water and jumped in without getting his boots wet. He landed with the grace of a fae, sinking down to sit on the seat.

I grinned. "If I'd tried that, I'd be on my ass in the water."

A tiny smile tugged at the corner of his mouth, and warmth bloomed within me.

He smiled so rarely that every curve of his lips felt like a gift. Especially when I thought about the context of his life. He'd been alive so damned long. And likely lonely for most of it. It felt crazy to think of someone as powerful and composed as Drakon being lonely, but he had been. I could feel it.

It made every smile I got from him precious. I tucked the memory of it away like a treasure.

He spun around on his seat to face the proper direction, then picked up the oars that had been tucked into the side of the boat and began to row.

Unable to help myself, I watched his muscles move beneath his shirt as he pulled on the oars. He was truly a living work of art. We glided silently across the water, and I turned to check how close we were to the island.

It appeared farther away than ever, though.

"That's strange." I frowned and glanced back at Drakon. "Do you see what I see?"

"What?" He looked over his shoulder and met my eyes, then his gaze traveled to the island. A frown creased his face. "The island appears farther away."

"Keep rowing."

He turned back and put even more force into his strokes. We didn't get any closer, however. Even though we made progress through the water, the island appeared to move farther away. "Shit. I don't remember this."

"There has to be a secret way to access it."

"I bet I would have known how once. Let me try to remember." I closed my eyes and focused my magic once more. It came even easier this time, my mind seeming to meld with the universe around me. Energy filled me, fresh and new.

How did I get to the island?

An image appeared in my mind—myself, as a child. I rode in this boat, though I couldn't see who manned the oars. I was leaning out over the edge of the boat and dangling my fingertips in the water. Magic sparked around my hand as the water rippled by.

"That's it." I opened my eyes and dipped my hand in the water. "The lake needs to know that someone with my bloodline is approaching."

"A clever protective charm."

After a moment, it became clear that the island was growing closer. "It's working."

I left my hand in the water as we traveled, the cool liquid chilling me to the bone. There was something about the water that I didn't like, giving me the strongest feeling that if we fell in, we'd never get out again.

Finally, we reached the island. Drakon gave one last heave of the oars and the bow of the boat crunched onto the pebble beach. I leapt out, narrowly avoiding the lapping waves, and he followed.

I stared up at the dead trees as Drakon pulled the vessel higher onto the beach.

"They were alive when I was here last. Their canopy shaded the island when I'd played." Now, they looked like skeletal hands reaching toward the sky.

I shivered. The island felt even more haunted than the mainland had. "Let's find this tomb and get the hell out of here."

6

Mac

I drew in a deep breath and tried to calm my racing heart. Something about being here made me feel like I'd just been given a shot of adrenaline.

I was close.

To my mother. To answers. To a past that I was becoming more afraid of with every moment I spent here.

Didn't matter.

I had to keep moving forward.

The island was dead silent. Not even the wind rustled the skeletal trees. I looked at Drakon. "Do you hear any animals in the underbrush?"

"No. I don't think there's a single living thing on this island."

"Except my mother."

"She's far away then, because I can't hear her."

The island itself was quite small and flat. I couldn't see all the way across, but it was clear there wasn't a building on it. "I think she must be underground."

"Do you know where?"

I shook my head and started forward. "I'll find it."

The pebble beach crunched underfoot as I made my way up onto the island. I'd mentioned underbrush to Drakon, but there really wasn't any. Just some dead bushes, their twisted branches looking as skeletal as the trees. Boulders dotted the island here and there. Following my instincts, I made my way to the center of the island.

Drakon followed, his footsteps silent but his presence comforting. No memories flowed into my mind as I walked, and I didn't go hunting for them. I didn't want to unless I needed them. As desperate as I'd been to remember my past, being here was curing me of that.

I wasn't sure I'd like what I found.

A few minutes later, we located a dark pit in the middle of the island. Stone stairs led down into it, and I stopped to stare. A shiver raced over my spine. "This must be it."

"Eerie looking."

I nodded. Dark shadows hovered in the depths, and

the stairs looked damp and worn. I sucked in a bracing breath, then walked down into the pit. The air chilled noticeably, and my eyes slowly adjusted to the gloom.

At the bottom, I found nothing.

"Shit." I crouched down and touched the pile of dirt that the stairs disappeared into.

"This is odd." Drakon's voice sounded right behind me, and I jumped.

"Someone filled it in." I frowned. "But why?"

"To keep people out?"

"Then why not fill it completely so the stairs are entirely hidden?"

"Fair point."

I sat on one of the lowest steps and stared at the dirt, thinking. "This is weird. Something isn't right."

"I've been getting that feeling since we arrived here."

"Agreed. But this is even weirder than everything else." I frowned. "We're on the wrong trail."

"You don't think your mother is on this island?"

"Oh, she is. I can feel her more strongly than ever. But I don't think this is the entrance." Something in my gut screamed it at me, and the magic that filled my soul was vibrating. Asking me to use it.

I closed my eyes and pressed my hands to the dirt wall at my side, trying to feel the energy of the earth. Trying to become one with it. Something about my new power worked best when I became joined to the world around me, when it felt like my atoms danced with those in my surroundings.

Where are you?

I pushed the questing thought out into the universe.

The answer came a moment later in my mother's faint, echoing voice. *Only one with our bloodline can enter.*

A memory slammed into my head—myself, as a child on this island. I'd explored every inch back then.

"This wasn't the entrance." I opened my eyes and stood, following a tug in my soul that directed me back up the stairs.

"Do you know where it was?"

"Maybe." I followed the pull, slipping past Drakon and climbing the stairs to the surface.

My magic sparked within me as I walked, following instinct as I headed toward another part of the island. Occasionally, I got flashes of what this place would have once looked like. Drakon followed behind me, silent and supportive.

When I found the patch of rocky ground, I stopped. "This is it."

"Really?" He stared down at the flat slabs of rock. "Is it an illusion? Or a door?"

"Illusion, I think." I stepped toward it and was hit with a blast of repellent magic that made me want to veer around the slab of stone. Putting my foot on it felt like a terrible idea. "You feel that?"

He nodded. "This has got to be the place."

I fought the urge to step away and tapped my toe against the stone. It disappeared, revealing a second stone staircase. I grinned. "There we go."

As I walked down the stairs, the sense of rightness filled me. This was it.

But it wasn't any less creepy than the other set of stairs. The air was damp and cold, the stairs slippery beneath my feet. Drakon followed, and we stopped in front of a heavy stone door at the bottom.

"I don't think this was here when I was a child. I recall tunnels, but no door."

"Perhaps it was added when your mother was locked away here."

The thought made my heart thunder. Could she really be alive behind this door? Everything felt so ancient and abandoned. "How has she survived all this time?"

"Has she?"

"She's calling to me in my mind. Visiting me. She's alive."

"Then it must be a spell. A powerful one."

I nodded. He was right. There were plenty of spells that could keep a person in a state of stasis, surviving in otherwise terrible conditions. "Did my father lock her in here?"

"I wouldn't put anything past him."

I shuddered, remembering his cold, reptilian personality. "I agree. He was definitely capable."

I ran my hand over the surface, trying to feel for a spell. For a way to open it.

Only our bloodline.

My mother's words echoed in my head.

I drew my sword from the ether and sliced my left palm. When the blood welled, I pressed it to the door.

Magic sparked, and I felt the spell break.

Quickly, I stashed the sword back in the ether and pressed both palms to the door, trying to push it open.

It didn't budge.

"It's not magic holding it anymore," I said. "It's just damned heavy."

Drakon joined me, putting all his strength to the task.

Slowly, the door creaked open, the stone dragging heavily against the dirt floor. Cold, stale air wafted out of the darkness, and I coughed.

A shiver of foreboding raced over me as I squinted into the gloom. It was impossible to see anything, and fear raced through me.

I'd never been afraid of the dark or of places like this.

"Are you all right?" Drakon asked.

For some reason, I confessed. "I think I'm scared of what I'll find."

"Your mother?"

"Yes. And the answers I'll get." I looked up at him, drawing comfort from his strong, calm presence. "This place is horrible. It was horrible before the disaster that cursed it, and it's even worse now."

He nodded. "It's a dark place, but you haven't been tainted by it. You'll come out of this as strong and bright as you've ever been."

"Bright?"

"Like the sun."

I blinked at him. "That's how you see me?"

The faintest flush crept over his cheeks, and my heart raced, delight rushing through me.

Drakon was *blushing.*

Holy fates, I was sure he'd never done that in his entire thousand years of life.

"Yes." His voice was slightly rough when he spoke, as if he were determined to get the words out. "You shine like the sun, a light in the darkness."

I swallowed hard, touched beyond words. "No one has ever said anything so nice to me."

"They should have." He cleared his throat and looked ahead. "We should enter."

I drew in a deep breath and turned away.

He was right. As much as I wanted to stand here with him and hear more, I couldn't.

The tomb beckoned, and I needed the answers that it contained.

"Here goes nothing." I stepped into the darkness, the cool air wrapping around me. My heart raced as I went deeper into the tunnel.

"Mac."

I turned.

Drakon was still at the entrance. "Aren't you coming?"

"I can't." He frowned, trying to step forward. An invisible wall stopped him, and I watched him fight against it. "The tomb is barred from me."

My mother's words flashed in my mind. "My mother said something about my bloodline, and this must be part of that."

"Come back and we'll find a way to break the spell. It's too dangerous."

"I'll be fine." And it didn't matter if it was too dangerous. I couldn't turn back now. "I'll be back."

"Mac!"

The worry in his voice made warmth flush through me.

He cared.

The idea made my heart race, and I tried to shove away all thoughts of Drakon.

As the tunnel grew increasingly dim, I drew my phone from my pocket and turned on the torch. It cast a bright white beam through the gloom, harsh and out of place in the ancient tunnel.

Faint memories rushed through me. As a child, I'd played here, giving myself a scare and a thrill as I'd run through the tunnels. There were rooms down here as well, but I couldn't remember where.

"Mother?" I called, my voice weak.

Was that what I'd called her? Or mom?

Neither felt natural, actually.

In fact, I had no idea what I'd called her. When I tried to dredge up the memory, nothing happened.

Weird.

I forced myself to call out, louder this time. "Mother! Where are you?"

The word still felt strange on my tongue, but I kept calling. The deeper I went, the more fiercely my magic sparked inside me. When I reached a large room, I stopped.

A figure stood on the far side, shadowy and still.

I'd found her.

7

Mac

"Daughter?" The voice was faint and familiar.

"Mother. You're here."

"Of course I am." She stepped forward, her face pale and her eyes tired. She looked just like she had in my vision—wispy blond hair pulled up behind her head and a long green dress that hung from her slim frame.

My heart thundered as I looked at her, waiting for emotion to fill me.

I should be feeling a rush of love, right?

Happiness?

I felt satisfaction at having found her, but not much else.

The woman who approached me was a stranger, and

the fact that I didn't remember anything about her—or even *feel* anything—made chills pop up over my body.

That couldn't be normal.

I should be elated to see her.

Especially since she appeared happy. As she approached, her face glowed with warmth and joy. "You came."

"Of course." I held out my arms, feeling like I should hug her.

When she didn't step into my embrace, I dropped them, weirdly grateful.

I didn't want to hug her. I knew I should want to, but I didn't.

"I'm still a stranger to you," she said. "I can see it in your eyes."

That was probably why she hadn't hugged me. Just reading me and respecting my boundaries. I appreciated it.

"You are." I rubbed my temple. "I wish I could remember. But it's fine. Let's get you out of here."

"I can't leave. Not yet."

Surprise flashed through me. "Wait, what?"

"I can't leave until Ludovic is dead."

Kill my father. On one hand, I didn't mind that much. He was downright evil, and I'd been trying to kill him almost since I'd met him. It needed to happen.

But hearing my mother say that I needed to kill my father was really effed up.

Was this what my family was?

No wonder I didn't want to remember.

But I had to. "Why not? What happened? How did you end up here?"

"Your father and I had a disagreement."

"What kind?"

"About you, actually." Her gaze traced over my face. "Your father wanted to use you for your power. I wanted you to be free."

"So he locked you in here."

"Hmm." Her face creased with anger. "And I've been stuck here for years, kept alive by a miserable spell that will only break when he is dead."

A spell—just as Drakon had said. "I'll get you out. I promise."

"Good. The first thing you must do is kill him. Then return here to me."

Hearing her repeat that I needed to kill my father made me grimace, but I ignored it. "What about my past? What am I? You said you had answers. What is the arcane order?"

"You will get your answers when you can find the heart in the forest."

"Where is that?"

"Only you will know. It will come to you."

Damn it, none of this was what I'd wanted. It was too many riddles. Why was it so damned hard to get a straight answer? "Surely you know what I am, at least."

"Not fully, no. Those answers can be found with the heart in the forest, and they will make you stronger. You will need that strength to defeat Ludovic, but you cannot rush the process."

Annoyance surged through me. I'd wanted more, damn it. "I've come all this way for one little bit of information?"

"It's not just any bit of information. And now that I've told you, your memory will be unlocked. The information will come to you."

My memories seemed to be linked to everything. "As soon as I started to remember, we became linked. Is this similar?"

"It is. Your memory will join you to your past. You just need to be brave enough to face it."

Brave enough.

My bravery was what had gotten me through life so far. Hopefully, it would help me once again.

"Find the heart so that you may embrace your magic. Then do what you must and return to me."

Again, a shiver raced over me. My life was seriously weird.

"Goodbye, daughter. I will see you soon." She stepped backward. The shadows of the tomb seemed to reach forward and envelop her, stealing her away from my sight.

I tried to follow, but a forcefield pressed against me. The tomb was trying to keep me out—I felt it in the core of my soul. If I forced my way past this barrier, I'd be trapped here with my mother.

"Damn it. Come back!"

There was only silence.

Shit, shit, shit.

This hadn't been what I'd expected.

Frustrated, I turned to leave, making my way back through the tunnels as quickly as I could. Every inch of my body felt like it crawled with spiders, and I couldn't wait to see the wide-open space above.

By the time I reached the exit, I was nearly vibrating with the desire to get out of there.

Drakon waited for me, his big form filling the entry. Light shined behind him, blinding me to the details of his features.

I hurried toward him and slipped from the tomb away from the cold darkness that was full of confusing half-answers about my past.

At the surface, he yanked me into a tight embrace. His warmth and strength surrounded me, a cocoon that blocked out the world and made me feel like I'd be protected forever. The concern all but vibrated from him.

"Don't do that again." His voice was rough against the top of my head.

"I'll do whatever I want." But the relief in his voice made warmth fill me.

He cared. And I *loved* that he cared.

"Stubborn woman." He pulled away, his jaw tightening as he shook his head, clearly disappointed in himself for caving to emotion.

I wanted to make him cave more often. It made me feel alive.

"Are you all right?" He let go of me, stepping back another few inches.

"I'm fine."

He nodded, looking like he wanted to wrap his arms around me once more. *Do it.*

But he didn't. "You haven't asked about my mother."

"Right. Of course." His eyes flashed, and from the tone of his voice I realized that he had forgotten about her.

He didn't care about her. He didn't care about any of this. He only cared about me. It felt like I could read all of that on his face, our bond linking us.

I reached for him and gripped his hand, unable to help myself. I wanted that connection.

I got more than I bargained for, however.

Pain shot through me, the feeling of my muscles tightening up and turning to stone. I gasped, stumbling backward. He reached out and caught me before I fell down the dark stairs.

He pulled me to safety, stopping just short of folding me into another embrace. "Mac, what's wrong?"

"I can feel what's happening to you." My stomach turned at the memory of the pain. The link between us had died, but it didn't matter. I'd never forget that horrible feeling. "I think it's our bond. Sometimes it lets me feel what you're feeling. The curse is advancing."

All expression wiped from his face, and his eyes darkened. "Don't worry about it."

"Are you crazy? Of course I worry about it. You remember what the witches said. When you turn to stone again, it will be the last time. And it feels like you're going to turn to stone any minute."

"I have a few days more."

"A few *days*? That's nothing." Panic and anger tightened their fists around my lungs, making my breath feel tight. "Why won't you drink from me? We have a solution, and you won't take it. It's crazy."

His jaw tightened as if he didn't want to speak.

"Take my blood. Please." The demand in my voice was hard as diamonds.

"I'll lose my immortality if I fall for you. And if I'm with you every day to drink your blood..."

I waited, wanting him to say it.

"I'll fall for you."

My breath caught. He'd said it.

And now that I'd heard it, I wanted it. I wanted a life with him. I wanted his love.

And he wanted his immortality.

"But... Hang on. If you don't drink from me, you'll turn to stone. Which is worse than a mortal life."

He opened his mouth, clearly wanting to argue the point. But he couldn't.

"What's the real reason you don't want to drink from me? Because it's not that bullshit about losing your immortality. You're too smart for that."

He gripped my hand. "Come on, we're going."

The ether pulled on me as he tried to transport me away. I fought it, my stomach lurching as it pulled at my muscles and bones. It hurt like hell to fight the tug of the ether, but I managed it.

I'm getting stronger. The realization hit me, but I stored it away for later. "I'm not going anywhere until you tell me what the real reason is. I know there's something else."

"We need to go."

"Tell me." I gripped his shirt collar and tried to shake him.

He didn't budge.

"I'll stay here all day."

"Fine." Frustration flashed on his face. "I don't deserve you, all right? That's the problem."

"Wait...what?" *That* wasn't what I'd expected.

"I'm all darkness, and you're light. I wasn't even born. I was made, and I've no idea why or by who. Probably to be a balancing force to the world—death to balance life. You don't deserve that."

"I don't think that's true at all. And it's stupid,

anyway. I don't care how you came to be—just that you *are.*"

He shook his head, clearly exasperated. "It's kind of you to say that, but it doesn't change anything."

"You don't believe me."

"Would you, if you were in my position?"

No, maybe not. He'd never known love. Not from parents, and likely not from anyone else. He'd been alone for a thousand years, and the enormity of that suddenly hit me.

Of course he couldn't believe himself worthy. Especially since he'd been created as a vampire, with all the violent urges that entailed. He had strength and self control now, but the stories about him made it clear he hadn't always had that.

He'd done terrible things, which likely made him doubt himself even more.

How was I supposed to fix that? How was I supposed to convince him he was worthy and that I wanted him when he was so determined to disbelieve me?

"I've told you what you want to know." Disgust sounded in his voice. "Be satisfied and let me take you from this place."

I nodded, knowing that the conversation was over. "Fine. But you *will* take my blood. I won't let you be entombed in granite."

He said nothing as he gripped my hand. The ether

tugged at us, pulling us away from my childhood home and spinning us through space.

When we arrived in the courtyard in front of the Shadow Guild tower, gratitude filled me.

My *real* home, not that horrible estate with foggy memories.

The sun was beginning to set over the city, and the faint sound of birds filled the air. The scent of oncoming rain was wonderfully familiar—this was England, after all—and my gaze ran over the tower and the rose bushes that climbed up the stone walls.

I should have felt this way when standing in front of my mother—family was home, after all.

And yet I hadn't. I only felt it here.

"You should rest," he said. "Did you learn anything pressing from your mother?"

He needed to rest. I could see it all over his face. Not that he was physically tired but confessing to his feelings had clearly taken a toll on him. He was pale, and his jaw was tight.

Drakon needed space.

"Not anything that can't wait until morning," I said. "We'll need to do some research anyway." I had no idea what the heart in the forest was.

"I'll be back then." He disappeared.

Suddenly, I was alone. The feeling of *home* diminished. It was still there, but not nearly as strong.

Shit.

Drakon was becoming my feeling of home. And if he turned to stone, I might never recover.

Since he'd refused to take my blood, did he really have a few days left? Cold fear iced my bones. What if he turned to stone while he was away from me? What if he had no time left?

"Mac?" Carrow's voice shook me from my horrible thoughts, and I turned to the tower.

My friend stood in the doorway, and I smiled. "Hey."

"Are you all right? You look pale."

"Yeah, I'm fine." I started toward her.

It was a lie, and from the look on her face, she knew it. Instead of pressing for answers, she just wrapped an arm around my shoulders and gave me a sideways hug. I leaned into her, grateful for the silent support.

"Come on," she said. "You could use a drink."

She stepped aside and I entered the tower, feeling the warmth of the hearth immediately. Gratitude rushed through me when I saw Seraphia and Beatrix sitting in front of the fire, takeaway containers piled in front of them.

My stomach grumbled audibly, and Beatrix held up a container. "Eat this."

"You're a hero. Thank you." I collapsed on the couch in front of her and took the container of Chinese food. As I shoveled noodles into my mouth, I could feel my friends' eyes on me.

Concern radiated from them, and as I slowed my

raccoon-like binging, I met their gazes. "You guys don't need to worry so much."

"Of course we do." Carrow scowled at me. "This is some heavy shit that's happening. How are you holding up?"

"Like a house of cards." I felt like I could collapse at any moment.

"You found your mother?"

"I did. And it was not what I expected." Guilt streaked through me. "I felt almost nothing for her." Maybe I was broken.

"Do you remember her?" Seraphia asked.

"Not really."

"Well, that's why then," Carrow said. "If you remember her, you'll feel something."

"I don't think that's the case, though. I should feel *something.* Anything. But I don't."

"What was she like?" Beatrix asked.

"A bit cold. She didn't hug me."

"Really?" Surprise flashed on Seraphia's face. "That's weird."

"Right? If she's my mother, wouldn't she want to hug me?"

"Maybe she's dysfunctional." Beatrix shrugged. "Bad with feelings, maybe?"

"That could be it." I couldn't blame her for being awkward. Hell, I was awkward a lot of the time, too. "Whatever her deal is, she gave me a clue. It's not much, but it's a start." I relayed everything she'd told me—the heart in the forest, the fact that she couldn't tell me what the Arcane Order was, and the way to release her from her prison.

"So we need to find a heart in a forest" Carrow frowned. "Maybe it's a metaphor for something?"

"It probably is," Seraphia said.

I leaned forward. "Maybe I can get us closer with my memory or my magic."

"That would help." Carrow nodded at Seraphia. "And if not, then this genius can figure it out."

"I'll start right away," Seraphia said. "If it's a known metaphor, I'll find it."

"Thank you." Gratitude welled within me. Seraphia was the town librarian, and there was nothing she couldn't find in her massive library. With my friends' help, we stood a chance.

8

Drakon

Cold wind whipped across my face as I strode toward my castle. I leaned into the bracing chill, letting it ground me in this reality. Though I'd returned home, I felt like my soul was still with Mac.

If I even had a soul.

The thoughts that occasionally haunted me in the darkness were running rampant through my head.

For centuries, I hadn't cared that I'd been created. That I very likely didn't have a soul.

But after meeting Mac, the thoughts had begun to haunt me. They'd crept into my mind only in the darkest hours, but it now felt like they'd taken up permanent residence inside my head.

I don't deserve her.

She was the only way I would survive, but it didn't matter. I couldn't shackle her to a creature such as myself.

My castle beckoned, and I climbed the stairs to the entrance. When I stepped into the enormous front hall, the usual feeling of comfort didn't rush over me. I'd created this place as my own perfect world, but I no longer cared about it.

The only thing that could warm me now was Mac.

Just the thought of her made pain streak through me. When I turned to stone, I'd be constantly away from her. Worse, I'd *know* that I was separated from her.

Death would be far preferable.

How much longer did I have left? Days? Hours?

My muscles felt stiff and tight, pain tightening around them. I could feel the curse getting its claws into me, and my time was limited if I didn't drink her blood again.

If only there were another way. But Orinthia had banished any hope of that. I was dying.

I'd told Mac that my immortality would disappear if I fell for her. I felt like it was already gone. I hadn't recognized when it had happened, but she'd stolen my heart.

It made me even more determined to protect her from myself. To give her the life of freedom she deserved, not one shackled to a beast.

My last act would be to rid the world of those who threatened her. Ludovic would have to die. And when he did, I could let the curse take me. Mac would be free.

Mac

The dream crept up on me, stealing through my subconscious like a thief. Except, it felt like a thief coming to return something that it had stolen.

Information.

Despite my slumbering state, I could tell that this was no ordinary dream. I had been afraid to fall asleep, but exhaustion had dragged me down.

Now, the dream demanded my attention, and I was helpless not to give it. There was truth in the dark forest. Massive trees soared around me, their bark blackened and rough.

Romania. The Black Forest.

Instinct told me that I was in Romania. And something was calling to me deep in the woods. It tugged at my soul, drawing me forward through the trees.

When the small stone building appeared in front of me, a sense of recognition flared. Built of pale stone, it was no larger than a cottage. The large wooden door appeared to be locked by a sturdy golden padlock, and I could feel that there was something within that I desperately needed to access.

The heart in the forest.

It was inside this building.

Heart pounding, I strode toward the little structure and tugged at the padlock. It didn't budge, and I had no skill for picking locks.

I turned back to the forest and looked around as if I would find something to help me.

A shadow lurked amongst the trees.

Drakon.

Though I couldn't see him, every nerve ending in my body lit up with recognition and desire. The strongest sense of need rushed through me. Not just physical, but emotional. Magical.

He could help me with the door. More than that, I needed him to be here. I wasn't sure why, but it was imperative that he be at my side.

We were linked, and I didn't want to fight it.

"Drakon." I reached out to him, trying to beckon him near.

He didn't respond, but someone else did.

"Daughter." Ludovic's voice sounded from behind me, and ice ran down my back.

No.

He couldn't be here. Not again.

I turned, spotting a shadow amongst the trees. It was vaguely man shaped, and a sense of evil drifted from it.

My father was here.

The shadow drifted toward me, and I stumbled backward, desperate to get away. It was too fast. Within seconds, it was upon me, wrapping around my limbs and tugging on me.

Like last time, the ether pulled hard, trying to steal me away.

Holy fates, my father could kidnap me from my dream—from my *bed.* Nothing was safe. I screamed, trying to tear myself away from the living nightmare.

The ether just pulled harder, and my mind went blank with panic.

I couldn't let him get me. If he did, I'd never survive.

Wake up!

Genevieve's voice cut through the dream, and I felt someone shaking me. I tore myself away from the vision, waking with a gasp.

A small black and white face peered down at me, concern glinting in dark eyes. *You were starting to disappear.*

"Thanks." I wiped a hand over my sweaty brow, wheezing from the pressure of Genevieve on my chest. "Can you get off of me?"

Are you sure? I'm holding you down so you don't disappear.

"I think the threat has passed. It's only when I'm asleep." I could still feel Ludovic's grip on me, but it was memory, not reality.

If you're sure...

"I heard screaming. Are you all right?" Eve's voice sounded from the doorway, and I looked over. Her hair was ruffled from sleep and her robe loosely knotted.

"Yeah." I dragged myself upright on the bed and gave her a play-by-play of both dreams and what I thought they meant.

Her face turned pale. "Shit. That's bad news."

"I know. Do you have anything to help? Something that might keep him from taking me?"

"Hmm." She pursed her lips as she thought. "I think I might have something that will help protect you. It won't be perfect, but it will tie you to this plane more, making it harder for Ludovic to steal you away."

"Thank you."

"Be right back." She turned and left.

I looked toward the window where the sky was beginning to lighten. The memory of my dream drifted back to me. Before Ludovic had appeared, I'd seen something valuable.

My mother's words echoed in my head — the heart in the forest.

Somehow, she'd triggered my memory once more, and the information had come to me in dreams.

"I know where I have to go."

Really? Genevieve blinked at me from her side of the bed. *Where?*

"Romania. But first I need to get Drakon. My dream made it clear that he needed to be there with me."

Lucky you. Her gaze turned wistful.

"Your crush hasn't abated, has it?"

No. And it's annoying, quite frankly, to pine after your friend's man.

I ruffled her head. "It's okay. I can share."

She brightened. *Run it by Drakon. Maybe we can be sister wives.*

There was way too much to unpack in that request, so I just said, "Sure thing."

Eve appeared back in the door, holding a small bottle aloft. "I've got the potion. Take it before you go to sleep, and it should help."

"Thank you." I climbed out of bed and took the potion. "You're the best."

"You're headed out? To Romania, I presume?"

"How can you tell?"

"You've got a glint in your eye, like excitement. That can only be because of Drakon, and he's in Romania."

"You've got me." Despite the residual nerves from my dream, I *was* excited to see Drakon. I had a feeling I would always be.

She pressed something else into my hand. "Since you're going to Romania, you're going to need this."

I looked down to see a transport charm. Eve was one of the few people capable of making them.

"You know I'm here if you ever need help."

"You're the best." I gave her a quick hug, and she left.

I hurried to the shower and cleaned up in record time. The outfit that I threw on didn't match—did green trousers go with a black sweater and leather jacket?

No matter.

I shoved the potion into the pocket of my trousers.

Genevieve stared doubtfully at me as I went to the door. *You're wearing that?*

"Yes." I tugged on orange trainers and knew I looked a mess. I hadn't even bothered to dry my hair.

I didn't care.

Finally, you're showing a sense of style.

My brows climbed halfway up my forehead. "Really?"

Really. You've been playing it safe too long. Fashion is about risk.

I looked down at myself. Yep. This had been a risk. "I'm going to find Drakon, then we're headed out to learn more about my past. I'll let you know if we need help."

Of course you'll need me.

I grinned as I slipped out the door. Oh, to have the confidence of a posh old badger.

By the time I made it to the courtyard in front of our tower, the morning sun was shining brightly, shedding the last bit of its warmth in the middle of this brisk fall day.

My heart thundered with anticipation as I chucked

the transport charm to the ground and stepped inside the silver cloud. As the ether sucked me toward Drakon's castle in Romania, visions of him flashed in my mind's eye.

I couldn't wait to see him.

As crazy as it sounded, I wanted to spend most of every day with him.

It was nuts.

When the ether spit me out in Romania, the cold wind whipped my hair back from my face. Gray clouds filled the sky, lending an ominous air. The castle loomed in front of me as lightning struck behind it. Dark clouds rolled across the sky, smelling of fresh rain.

I shivered and hurried to the castle door. The massive wooden thing appeared foreboding from the outside, reflecting the interior. Drakon didn't have a knack for welcoming home decor. No surprise.

As I reached the top step and raised my hand to pound on the door, it swung open. I stepped back, startled to see Drakon in front of me.

He was as handsome and imposing as ever, making my heart race even faster. I had to tilt my head back to meet his surprised gaze.

"Did you see me from the window?" I asked.

"No. I was coming to find you."

Warmth rushed through me. "Really?"

He nodded briefly. "I'm going to help you catch Ludovic."

"Thank you."

"Why are you here?"

"I had a dream that showed me where to go to find out more about my past. My mother said that was the first step in defeating Ludovic."

He nodded. "Where do we need to go?"

I couldn't help the small smile that tugged at my lips. *We.* I loved how quickly he added himself to my life. How he *specifically* added himself into situations where I needed help.

"Not too far from here, actually. I need to go to a place called The Black Forest. It's in Romania. I'm sure of it."

Surprise flashed on his face again. "That name came to you in a dream?"

I nodded. "Why do you seem so surprised?"

"I haven't heard anyone speak of that place in centuries. Even when people spoke of it, most thought it wasn't real. It was just a place of legend for them."

"What did they say about it?"

"That it was dangerous. The forest is ruled by a vampire queen and inhabited by deadly magical creatures. The monsters there obey her—for the most part. She considers herself its guardian. We'll have to get her permission to enter, or they'll kill us on sight."

"Surely you can do that? You're Drakon."

"Normally that would get me certain privileges. But with Tatiana... She's not a fan of mine."

He said it in a way that implied they had a rocky history. A romantic history, from the way his gaze moved to the side.

Unexpected jealousy streaked through me, followed swiftly by annoyance.

Damn it. I didn't like being jealous. I never was—not normally, at least. It was dumb as hell and a total waste of time.

Drakon made everything different.

"Well, we have to go anyway," I said. "Maybe you can still work your magic."

He nodded, but skepticism flashed in his gaze. "We'll find a way in, even if Tatiana doesn't permit us access."

"Can you take us?"

"I can." He reached for my hand, and I shivered as his fingers closed around mine.

I could feel the stiffness in his limbs and frowned up at him. "You don't want to touch me, do you?"

Pain flashed across his face. "It's not a matter of *want.* I want to spend the rest of eternity touching you." Surprise filled his eyes, as if he couldn't believe he'd admitted that.

I couldn't believe he had either. He'd spent so long holding himself apart from me—he was *still* trying. Quite desperately, from the tense set of his shoulders and the pain on his face.

And yet, the words still escaped him.

"I just can't." The words came out on a rough whisper. "It's too dangerous."

He was going to help me and then disappear. I could feel it like I could feel the breath in my lungs.

I wouldn't let that happen.

"Let's go." He squeezed my hand, and the ether tugged on me.

It spun us through space, spitting us out a few moments later. Drakon let go of me as soon as he could, and the loss of his touch ached.

I spun in a circle, taking in our surroundings. The weather was similarly ominous here, with heavy dark clouds and the scent of rain on the air.

Fields spread out to one side, forest on the other. The huge trees had pitch-black bark, and the leaves were a deep green. A wide, rocky river roared by in front of the forest, and a fortress built of honey colored stone sat on its banks. It reminded me a bit of Drakon's castle.

"Very vampiric," I muttered. These Transylvania vampires did not disappoint.

"Come. She'll know we're here." He strode toward the castle, and I followed.

Light rain began to fall from the sky, and I hunched my shoulders as I flipped up my collar. Drakon strode up to the fortress gate like he owned it. The massive wall surrounded a huge castle with multiple round turrets, and the gate itself was built of black wood studded with silver spikes.

As we neared it, magic sparked on the air.

"A barrier," he said. "It senses when people arrive."

I shivered. The barrier felt prickly and threatening—a spell meant to intimidate visitors.

It was working.

When we reached the gate, Drakon pounded on it. An ominous boom sounded with every blow of his fist, and the rain came harder. It stung my skin, cold and sharp. Drakon seemed impervious to it.

When the gate swung open, I stepped back, startled. A massive black panther stood in front of us, fur sleek and gleaming. Red eyes watched us with deep intelligence, and it was clearly no ordinary cat. I'd have said it was a shifter, but that didn't seem quite right either.

A moment later, magic sparked, and the panther transformed into a beautiful woman with jet black hair and red eyes. Her crimson and black gown clung to her body and flared out at the base.

The vampire queen. It had to be.

Power radiated from her in waves that took my breath away. Her gaze narrowed on Drakon, the fire in her eyes flaming bright. "You. I didn't think you'd have the balls to come back."

He smiled, though there was no warmth in it. More heat flashed in her eyes, as if she'd been expecting that response.

She *liked* it, I realized. Whatever was going on

between them had a lot of history. I frowned, unable to help the second slight stab of jealousy.

Ugh, what was my problem?

Drakon brought out the worst in me. Probably because he wasn't really mine, even though I wanted him to be.

"Who did you bring?" The vampire queen's tone was bored, but when her gaze landed on me, interest flickered in her eyes. "Well, well. You look like someone I know."

"Well I don't know you." I stepped forward and extended my hand. "I'm Macbeth O'Connell."

She looked at my hand, amusement flashing on her face, then seemed to decide *oh, what the hell* and extended her own hand to shake mine.

A current of electricity passed between us as we made contact, and interest flashed in her eyes. "Yes, it seems I might have been mistaken. You aren't boring after all."

"Not all the time, at least."

She ignored the joke, and I got the impression she wasn't one for humor. "I feel like I should know you. And yet, I don't. Why is that?"

"I keep to myself. But we're here because we need to get into the Black Forest."

"Oh, do you now?" Amusement glinted in her eyes, and I frowned. *Shit.* That was not the response I'd been hoping for. "I'm not sure you're worthy."

"Let me prove myself."

Her gaze moved to Drakon. "What about him?"

"Him, too. He can do it."

She scoffed lightly, and irritation shot through me. Of course Drakon was worthy. I was certain he'd prove more worthy than me, whatever the task was. I opened my mouth to tell her so, but she turned and walked back into the main courtyard in front of her castle.

"I'll meet you later this evening." Her words echoed over her shoulder, followed by another flash of magic. She transformed back into a panther and stalked away.

Huh.

I looked at Drakon. "So, do we follow her or..."

"No." A voice cut in from the courtyard in front of us before Drakon could answer, and a man materialized, pale and drawn looking. His paper-thin skin appeared to be stretched tightly over sharp bones and was white as flour. Pale yellow eyes watched us keenly, and I shivered.

He wasn't human. Nor was he any other kind of supernatural I'd ever seen before.

Was he a ghoul?

I'd only heard of the creatures that preferred to live underground. They tended to keep to themselves, but that wasn't what gave them their poor reputation. No, that came from the fact that they ate the flesh of the dead—preferably stolen from graves under a full moon.

"I'll show you to your rooms." The slender man turned and stalked away, his gait uneven and jerky.

Yep, a ghoul.

Drakon walked close by my side as we made our way through the courtyard toward the tall, ornate castle. Dark glass covered the windows, and black roses climbed up the stones.

The ghoul led us through the main door into a moderately sized entry hall. Silk papered the walls, and a crystal chandelier shed a sparkling glow on the ornate space. A plush rug cushioned our footsteps, and artwork done in splashes of violent red covered the walls.

I squinted at it.

Yuck—I wasn't entirely convinced it wasn't blood.

The ghoul led us up a spiral staircase to a massive bedchamber on the third floor. Like the entryway, it was ornately decorated. A huge fourposter bed graced the space, and a large hearth flickered with brilliant flames. Two armchairs sat in front of the fireplace.

The ghoul slipped away silently, and six maids in black uniforms streamed into the room, chattering amongst themselves. Once inside, they stopped and stared at me.

"Oh dear." The one in the center tutted as she looked at me, shaking her head in dismay. "We have our work cut out for us."

9

Mac

"We have our work cut out for us?" I repeated the maid's words, feeling my eyebrows climb halfway up my forehead. "You're not talking about me, are you?"

"We're certainly not talking about *him*." She gave Drakon an appreciative look. "He's perfect."

They weren't wrong. But still... "I don't need any work."

All six maids laughed as if I'd said the funniest thing they'd ever heard. If their response was anything to go by, I could have sold tickets at the biggest stadium in London for a comedy show.

"I'm serious." I crossed my arms over my chest and glared.

"Sure, sure." The leader hustled around me.

I turned and watched her walk toward an enormous copper bathtub. I hadn't noticed it before, but it was a glorious monstrosity of luxury. It sat in front of a window with a beautiful view of the river outside.

The maid waved her hand over the tub, and steam curled up from it.

"Okay, maybe I'm interested." The tub looked divine. I just had to find a way to get some privacy from Drakon.

"Good." The leader turned to look at me. "Because there's no way the queen would have an audience with you while you look like that."

"She didn't mention a problem earlier."

"Not to you." She shared a look with the women behind me, and I heard them titter.

"Oh, whatever." I rolled my eyes, knowing it was childish but unable to help myself.

"Come now." She gestured, and the maids gathered around me.

Shoving me toward the tub, they removed my clothes. They were *fast*, and before I knew it, I was naked at a jay bird.

Crap.

I looked back over my shoulder at Drakon, but he'd taken a seat in front of the fire and stared into the orange flames. There was a stiffness to his shoulders, however, that suggested he was acutely aware of what was going on.

Shivering, I climbed into the tub and sank into the divine warmth. It soaked into my muscles, relaxing me like a drug.

One of the maids opened the windows slightly, and a fresh breeze rushed over my face. It smelled like the forest and a fresh, clean river. I sucked it deeply into my lungs, enjoying the sound of the river rushing by below.

This was heaven. "I could stay like this for a hundred years."

"Well, you can't." The lead maid nodded to the women behind me, and I felt a hand on the top of my head.

It shoved me down under the water. I barely resisted sucking it into my lungs. Fortunately, they weren't holding me down. I surged upright, sputtering as I gasped in air.

"What the hell was that for?" I demanded.

"Need to wash your hair." The leader grinned.

One of the maids handed me a crystal goblet full of sparkling golden liquid.

I took it, sniffing suspiciously.

"Just champagne." The leader bustled around to stand behind me.

I sipped, feeling like I'd need the wine if the beginning of this bath was an indication. As the women got to work washing my hair and scrubbing my skin, I couldn't help but look at Drakon.

Was he noticing me?

Definitely.

His shoulders were even stiffer than before, and his fist was clenched. It was weird as hell to be given a bath like a child, but he was a good distraction.

Look at me.

As if he'd heard my silent plea, his head turned toward me. Heat flashed in his eyes, and I felt it shoot through me, pooling at my core. I took a bracing sip of cold champagne, but it did little to douse the flames within.

Thank fates there was an army of maids here. They moved in front of me, blocking my view of Drakon.

For the best.

I turned my head to look out the window, catching sight of the beautiful river. It was wide and crystal clear, the water rushing over huge boulders. Beyond it, the Black Forest loomed.

A shiver raced over my skin.

It was one of the scariest places I'd ever seen, and I was about to beg my way into it.

Why couldn't my mother have told me that I'd find the answers at Disney World or the beach? Or at least someplace not quite so scary.

"Out, out, out!" The leader poked my shoulder, then waved a hand over the water.

It disappeared, and I shivered. Damn it, I'd wanted another hour at least.

One of the maids snatched the glass of champagne

from my hand and I stood. A cool breeze rushed over my naked skin, and I was intensely aware of Drakon's presence.

I glanced over, but he was staring into the flames once more.

"Here." One of the women handed me a towel, and I wrapped it around myself.

"Hurry up, we have a lot of work to do!" The leader bustled around me as I stepped out of the tub.

The next twenty minutes were a whirlwind as they fussed with my hair and face. I had no idea what they were doing, but I had a feeling I was going to look like a movie star when they were done.

Hopefully.

Or I'd look like a clown.

When they brought out a blood red satin dress, I felt my jaw drop. "Am I supposed to wear that?"

"No, he is." The leader nodded toward Drakon, then laughed.

"Ha ha." I stepped toward the woman holding the dress and touched the fabric. It was smooth and rich under my hands, and I felt my heart pound. I wasn't into clothing, but *anyone* would be into a dress like this. It felt like it had to have cost a million pounds.

"The queen only dines in style," the leader said. "She insists that her guests be appropriately clothed as well."

Within minutes, I was zipped into the dress and

feeling like a goddess. When they brought in a long mirror to give me a look at myself, I gasped.

I really did look like a movie star. Or a princess. My hair gleamed like gold, falling in heavy curls over my shoulder. The paint on my face was subtle but divine, highlighting my features so that I was more beautiful than I'd ever been.

As for the dress...

I couldn't believe how it fit so perfectly. It showed just the right amount of cleavage and clung to me in a way that revealed curves I didn't know I had.

"Well?" The leader directed her words toward Drakon. "What do you think?"

He turned toward me, surprise flashing on his face. Desire followed, and he cleared his throat. "You look lovely."

My gaze met his, and the current of heat that traveled between us made my chest tighten.

"Are you coming to dinner?" I asked.

"No." The lead maid shook her head. "Just you. He will wait here."

It was for the best. If he came, I'd spend the whole night trying not to stare at him, and I couldn't afford to be distracted.

"Come now." The leader bustled me out of the room, and I gave him one last glance over my shoulder, gratified to see him watching me leave.

The maids led me through the enormous castle. As I

walked, I tried to memorize the way from my room, but there were so many twists and turns that it soon became impossible.

The place was magnificent, though. If you were into fancy stuff, at least. Silk wallpaper covered the walls, and my footsteps were cushioned by thick rugs.

We climbed a wide spiral staircase that extended several stories upward. Finally, we arrived at the top of a tower. The fresh night breeze rushed over my face, and I drew in a bracing breath as I took in our surroundings.

Though it had grown dark, there was still plenty of light shed by the moon. The clouds parted to reveal the glowing orb and a canopy of bright stars. In the distance, the Black Forest loomed as a shadow.

A long, gleaming wooden table dominated the center of the roof. Though it was set with two dozen place settings, there was only one person sitting at it.

The queen occupied the chair at the end, and her eyebrows rose as she looked at me. "Good. I thought you would clean up nicely. I'm pleased to see that I was correct."

"Oh, this old thing?" I gestured to the dress.

The corner of her lip twitched. It wasn't a full laugh, but it was close. Unfortunately, humor wouldn't get me access to the Black Forest.

"Come, sit." She gestured to the seat next to her, and I joined her as the maids melted away.

Footmen lined the walls around us, but they stood

so silent and still that the queen and I might as well have been alone.

She handed me a glass of red wine, and I took it. The liquid gleamed ruby red under the dim light, and I stared at it, worry flashing through me.

"Don't worry," she said. "It's just Cabernet. Not blood."

It sure looked like blood.

"I promise." She smiled, and there was something cold about it that made me uncomfortable. "Blood is served on tap here, never out of glasses." She snapped her fingers, and one of the footmen shot off the wall and disappeared through the door.

A few moments later, he appeared with a young man dressed in a dark velvet suit. The two hurried forward, and the young man knelt at the queen's side, raising his wrist. Anticipation gleamed in his eyes, and it was clear that he didn't mind his job as a walking buffet.

"Thank you, Clarence." The queen nodded at the footman, then looked at me. "Cheers."

She gripped the young man's wrist and raised it to her mouth before sinking her fangs into his flesh. Pleasure flashed across his face, and he swayed a bit.

Though the man appeared willing, the scene still made me uncomfortable. Drakon never would have made me uncomfortable like this.

The vampire queen withdrew her mouth. After

licking the blood from her fangs, she said, "He would have, once. He was shameless back then."

Shock flashed through me. "You can read my mind?"

She nodded. "One of my many talents." She gestured to the forest beyond. "It is one of the reasons I am the queen of all you see."

Her magic radiated from her, thick with power. This was not a woman I wanted to mess with. But the lure of information about Drakon was too tempting to resist. "So he's changed a lot, then?"

She nodded. "Immensely so. And all because of you."

"How can you sound so certain about that?"

"I can feel it, of course. You and Drakon—there's something there. Something intense."

"Nothing that we should pursue." According to him, at least.

She laughed. "As if you'll have a choice in that matter."

"I determine my own fate. Not some magical force." And what I wanted was him.

"I knew I liked you." She waved her hand dismissively toward the man who had served as her dinner, and he hurried away. "But you can't fight fate, and you two positively stink of it."

"You can smell it?"

She shrugged. "Smell it, feel it. I don't know quite how to describe it. But it is impossible to ignore."

"We're mates."

"I suspected as much." She laughed softly. "The powerful Drakon, finally brought low."

"I don't think anything would bring him low."

"You could." She sighed. "I tried, of course, once upon a time. I needed a king for my court." She gestured to the land around us. "I thought he would be perfect for it."

"He disagreed?"

She nodded. "Vehemently. Oh, he was happy to visit for a party every now and again, but he wouldn't make it permanent."

I didn't want to think about what those parties entailed. It was clear from her voice that they had been crazy. "Did he say why?"

"He was still sowing his wild oats, I believe."

I grimaced, not liking the ancient phrase. "He was young?"

"Oh, eight hundred or so. He was once the terror of this region. Gave Vlad the Impaler a run for his money."

Vlad the Impaler. Grey, now known as the Devil of Darkvale and Carrow's mate.

"Another one who has changed, yes?" The queen's eyebrows rose. "Because of a woman."

It was true. The Devil of Darkvale was still scary as hell, but he had definitely mellowed. He and Carrow had a different story than Drakon and I, however. "There's no hope for us. No future."

The vampire queen nodded wisely. "Because of the curse."

"What do you know of it?"

"No more than you or he."

Damn. I hadn't truly thought she'd be able to give me a cure, but hope was hard to resist.

"But let's get down to business." She leaned forward, her gaze keen on me. "You want to go into the forest. To learn something about yourself?"

I nodded, wondering if she could see more. Did she know what I was?

"No." She shook her head. "But I believe you're the one we've been waiting for."

"Waiting for me? Why?"

"I do not know. The legends speak of a great power that was meant to return here."

Return. But I didn't recall having been here.

Another life.

It felt impossible, but it was the only explanation.

"Are the legends written down anywhere?" Maybe they'd give me the answers I sought.

"Not in a book. They are from artwork in an ancient church. Would you like to see?"

I nodded, and she waved her hand. The world spun around me, going bright and silvery with magic. When things finally slowed and I could focus my eyes, I realized that we were inside an ornate old church.

The building itself was built of wood, but the art on

the walls gleamed with golden leaf and bright paints beneath the chandeliers that held hundreds of candles.

"Are we really here?" I stood from my chair and walked slowly toward one of the walls, my gaze riveted by the painting there.

"No. It is an illusion, faithfully recreated."

I wanted to believe her, desperately so. Because that meant this place held answers. The images on the walls were detailed enough that I was sure they had to reveal information about me.

As I got close enough to make out the details, that suspicion was confirmed. The woman who'd been painted on the wall looked like me.

I felt the queen's presence at my shoulder. "See? It's you."

I nodded slowly, taking in the scene in front of me. The woman—myself—was arriving in the Dark Forest. She looked weary, and there was no indication of great magic.

I followed the murals around the room, tracing the woman's journey as a man appeared.

Drakon.

There was little about him, but it was clear he was important. The murals were damaged in some places, and I didn't gain any new information until the last one.

The woman entered a small stone building in the forest.

The building I'd seen in my dream.

It had to be.

The heart that my mother told me to seek had to be in that building. Was it a tomb? It made sense if it contained a body part.

When she left, she glowed with power. The magic all but vibrated from the mural, sparking against my skin.

My heart raced as I pointed to the image. "Do you know where that place is?"

"I do not. No one does, though we've searched the entire forest."

"Shit." Despair clutched at my heart. Had it been destroyed?

"It's there," the queen said. "Just because we can't find it doesn't mean it's not."

I clung to her words like a lifeline. I would find the tomb. I had to.

"No one remembers anything about this woman?" I asked, nodding toward the mural.

"No. Which is odd, given how important I think she was. I can feel it in my gut, like an ancient knowledge that has followed me. And yet, we don't know who she is."

"That's so strange."

"Indeed. It's as if she'd been wiped from our memories."

Wiped from our memories.

A shiver raced over my skin. I'd forgotten my own

memories. There was too much of that going around—it was suspicious.

"I'll get to the bottom of it." I turned to her. "Am I worthy of entering the forest?"

"We must see."

I frowned. "But you said—"

"Yes, I think you're important. But you still need to prove yourself."

10

Mac

The vampire queen smiled at me, her eyes sparkling with cunning. She waved her hand and the world swirled around me once more, the ether carrying me away from her. It spit me out in the courtyard in front of the Shadow Guild tower.

I blinked.

What the hell was I doing here?

The sky above was dark. Clouds drifted in front of a bright moon, casting dappled shadows on the stone tower.

Annoyance surged through me. I'd thought she'd said I would get to prove myself. Yet she'd sent me home like I'd already failed.

And she'd kept Drakon.

None of this seemed right.

I started toward the tower, determined to get a transport charm from Eve and return to the queen's castle. She'd grant me entrance to the Black Forest, no matter what it took.

As I neared the tower, I noticed smoke curling up from the roof. I frowned, squinting at it. There wasn't a chimney on that part of the roof.

Dread unfurled within me.

The smoke grew thicker, and brilliant orange flames burst through the windows. Glass shattered, flying outward in a glittering explosion. Fire licked up from the windows, eating away at the rose vines.

My friends.

Fear exploded within me, and I raced forward. Screams sounded from inside, horribly familiar. Carrow and Eve, Beatrix and Seraphia. Even Quinn was there.

They were all inside.

Shit, shit, shit.

There was so much fire—how could I possibly get to them all?

Doubt crept in, but I shoved it away.

As I neared, another explosion tore through the building. Jets of flame shot from the windows, and the force of it threw me backward. Cold fear mixed with the heat that scorched my skin.

It was an impossible inferno.

The screams sounded again and hope flared.

They were still alive.

I scrambled upright and staggered toward the blazing building. It was entirely engulfed now, the flames billowing from the door.

How was I supposed to get in there to help them?

My new magic. There had to be something there I could use.

Come on, damn it.

I shook my hands, trying to call upon my strange new power. I'd discovered crazy new gifts in the last couple weeks—surely one of those gifts would protect me while I went inside to help my friends.

And yet, my magic stayed dormant inside me. No matter how desperately I tried to access it, nothing happened. My soul was as cold and dead as a tomb.

By the time I reached the front door of the tower, I still hadn't found a power that would help me rescue them.

I just wasn't strong enough. Wasn't worthy.

It didn't matter.

I still had to try.

I waited until the flames in the doorway died down briefly, then pulled my shirt up over my mouth to filter out the smoke and plowed through the front door. Fear turned my limbs to jelly as I staggered through the main room. No one was within, and flames licked up the walls and devoured the furniture.

The heat stole my breath as I fought my way toward the stairs and started up a narrow path through the flames. I could make it. I had to.

"Carrow!" I screamed. "Eve! Beatrix! Seraphia!"

There was no response, and the fear nearly took me to my knees.

No.

If I went down, I'd never get back up. And my friends would die here. I couldn't let that happen.

I steeled myself against the heat and the terror and kept going, dragging myself up the stairs to the second level.

"Carrow!" I tried to scream her name, but the words came out on a whisper. My throat was raw from the smoke and my skin felt blistered.

I staggered down the hall, my steps getting wobblier and wobblier as I went.

Unworthy.

I'd never be strong enough to save them.

The agony of loss nearly suffocated me, growing stronger when my legs gave out and I went to my knees. I could still hear them screaming, and I tried to claw my way down the hallway toward the sounds. Flames licked toward me from the walls, but I didn't feel them.

Must get to them.

Panic kept me going, even when my vision started to black out.

When strong arms picked me up and cradled me

against a warm chest, a sense of safety rushed over me, quickly followed by anger.

"No," I croaked. "I have to find them."

"I'm getting you out of here." Drakon's voice echoed with concern.

"No." The steel in my tone made him stop. "We have to find them. *Have to.*"

"Fine." He bit out the word. "We'll search. Quickly."

Hope flared in my chest as he strode forward. But before we could make it toward the next door, the ether sucked us in and spun us through space.

"No!" I tried beating at his chest. "You bastard! Take us back!"

The ether spit us out in the cool, dark air of Romania. I sucked in fresh air, my lungs and head clearing.

Rage shot through me as I pounded on Drakon's shoulders. "Put me down and take me back!"

I couldn't *believe* he'd betrayed me like that, taking me away from my dying friends.

"Bastard!"

"It wasn't me." He set me down, gripping my shoulders and shaking me until I looked at him. "I didn't transport us out of there."

Disbelief raced through me, but he sounded so sincere. And confused.

"Then who?"

"I did." The vampire queen's voice sounded behind me, and I spun around to face her.

"Let me go back," I begged. "They're dying."

"It was an illusion. They're fine."

"An...illusion?" I scrubbed a hand over my face. Of course. She'd said I was being tested. Immediately, my panic faded, though my heart kept pounding. "You chose a good test. It was bad enough that panic made me think it was real."

Her lips pursed as she nodded, her narrowed gaze on Drakon. "How the hell did you manage to get into the illusion? You shouldn't have even been able to get to her."

"I felt her. Of course, I went to her." His hand gripped mine, the first time he'd ever shown such genuine public affection.

Warmth flushed through me, even though I knew that things between us were probably impossible.

No. I didn't want to think like that. Not any longer. There had to be a way.

"You shouldn't have been able to find her inside of my illusion, though." The queen crossed her arms over her chest. "It's impossible."

"Apparently it's not. Nothing can keep me from her."

"Nothing but the curse that will turn you to stone." The vampire queen looked between us. "Fate is powerful, though. You two are clearly meant to be together. If you can find a way."

I desperately wanted to find a way. Perhaps if I could get into the forest and find the heart, I could find a way to be with Drakon. My dream had suggested that it contained answers about us.

And yet, I'd failed the challenge.

"Let me try again," I begged. "I know I failed, but I can prove myself worthy."

"Failed?" Surprise flashed on her face.

"I didn't fail?" Hope flared. "But how? I didn't rescue my friends. I couldn't access my magic to save them."

The queen shrugged. "That's just life. Everyone knows you can't always win. Saving everyone is impossible." Her gaze moved to Drakon, and I knew what she was thinking. *You can't save him.* But damn it, I'd prove her wrong.

"It wasn't about saving them," she continued. "It was about the fact that you were willing to try in the face of certain death… That's what matters. It's your bravery that makes you worthy—not your skill."

Bravery.

That was something I'd always had, a foolhardy desire to throw myself into danger when I thought the situation called for it.

People had called me reckless for it. Stupid. Said I'd get myself killed.

And maybe I would. But right now, that quality had saved me. Maybe I wasn't so unworthy after all.

"Do you know what my magic is?" I asked. "What I am?"

She shook her head. "I do not. You haven't mastered it yet, but it doesn't matter."

"It sure feels like it matters. I don't know if I can face Ludovic with just what I have now."

"You probably can't. Even *I've* heard of that bastard. But I think you might be able to find answers in the forest. You may go tomorrow once the sun rises."

"Thank you." True gratitude welled within me.

Drakon

Mac and I walked back to our suite, the air thick with tension. I'd spend the entire night alternating between worry and desire. It was impossible to get the image of her in the bath out of my mind, but I'd started to feel like a real bastard when she had to leave to face Tatiana. The vampire queen wouldn't hurt her, but the trials had the potential to be dangerous.

They had been, and somehow, I'd felt it when she'd been in danger. The connection between us was so intense that it worked even when we were apart. I'd been so desperate to reach her, to help her, that the ether had sucked me in and transported me to her.

When I'd seen the Shadow Guild tower burning, my heart had nearly broken through my ribs. The heat had felt real as I'd raced up the stairs, and when I'd finally seen her at the top, collapsed, I'd felt like *I* was dying.

Thank fates I'd made it in time.

We arrived at the bedroom too soon. I was still vibrating with emotion—a first for me—and I'd hoped to get better control of myself. She slipped through the doorway in front of me, leaving a cloud of intoxicating scent behind her. I drew it deeply into my lungs, unable to stop myself from watching the way the silk dress moved on her body.

I wanted her more than I'd ever wanted anything in my life.

Desire gripped me, followed by hunger.

It was dangerous.

Everything about her was dangerous.

When she turned to me, she was only a couple steps ahead, so close that she took my breath away. Her eyes were bright, and her cheeks were flushed. "Thank you for coming for me. I didn't say it earlier, but I should have."

She raised a hand, tentative at first, then laid it on my chest.

My heart clutched, the contact enough to make me stop breathing entirely.

I felt like a man dying in the desert, and she was the oasis in the distance.

All of my good reasons for resisting her flew from

my mind. I'd wanted her for so long, the need ravenous inside me. To touch her, to kiss her...

It was more than I could resist.

The heat of her hand on my chest burned me, but not as hot as the desire in her eyes.

"Drakon." She murmured my name, a question at the end of it.

Yes.

Yes, I wanted her. More than I wanted my next breath, and I could no longer fight my desire. Just a taste couldn't hurt. I knew that was a damned lie even as I thought it, but I clung to it all the same.

"Tell me to stop, Mac." My voice was no more than a growl, brought low by the desire that threatened to consume me.

"Keep going." She leaned toward me, her lips parting as her hand slid up my chest to cup my neck.

I couldn't say no to that. Who could?

With a low groan, I leaned down to press my lips to hers.

Ambrosia.

Even sweeter than before.

A low moan escaped her as she slipped her tongue into my mouth. The slick heat of it stole my mind away, and I groaned, clutching her hips and pulling her toward me. My mouth was ravenous on hers as she pressed her body flush to mine. Every soft inch of her curves cradled every hard inch of me.

"Let me taste you," I begged. "Please."

"You are," she gasped. "But you have permission for whatever you want."

The words were all I needed to hear. I hoisted her up until her long legs wrapped around my waist. Heat spiked through me, and I bit back a groan.

In several long strides, I had her to the nearest surface—a table by the door. I sat her upon it, and she gasped with surprise, breaking away from our kiss to meet my eyes.

I just grinned at her and sank to my knees, flipping her silk skirts up over her thighs.

"Drakon." Her voice was breathy as she sank her hands into my hair. "What are you—"

I pressed my lips to the front of her undergarments, breathing in her heavenly scent. She moved against my mouth, a low sound of pleasure filling the room.

I couldn't wait any longer. I'd wanted to taste her for centuries—at least, it felt that way.

Quickly, I divested her of her undergarments and pressed my lips to her soft folds. Silken dew greeted me, and I kissed her like I would die if I didn't.

I was sure I was.

"Drakon, I can't last like this." Her hands clutched at my hair as her hips moved against my lips. She seemed unable to control herself, and I loved it.

The moments melded together into an eternity that was too short. I could have lived like this.

Yet my body wouldn't tolerate that. As her desire wound higher and higher, so did mine. By the time her pleasure overtook her, and she was going over the edge, I was ready to follow. Like a lad, I lost my self-control and let the pleasure overwhelm me, unable to stop the waves that pulsed through me.

Every moment that passed was the most amazing of my life, until the one where Mac slumped over me and sighed. "That was incredible. Best ever."

Satisfaction shot through me, and I rose to my feet, sweeping her into my arms. "I don't know about you, but I could use a bath."

11

Mac

I woke the next morning with my limbs wrapped around Drakon's. He was strong and warm beneath me, his chest rising and falling with a steady rhythm. Memories of last night filled my head. Heat flushed through me, a combination of embarrassment and desire.

Last night had been...phenomenal.

There were no words for it.

After our explosive experience on the table near the door, we'd taken a shower together. Despite the joyous energy running through me, exhaustion had overtaken my body. I'd barely had enough time to take the potion that Eve had given me to protect me from Ludovic while

I slept. Drakon had carried me to bed, where we'd slept in each other's arms until sunrise.

How I wished we could spend the day in bed. I'd give anything to lounge around with him.

A knock sounded at the door, sharp and loud. The voice that filtered through was no-nonsense and commanding. "It is time."

Drakon opened his eyes, immediately alert. When his gaze met mine, heat flashed briefly on his face. Then the knock sounded again, and his expression cleared.

"We're coming," he called out, glaring at the door. "Leave us the bloody hell alone."

The knocking stopped abruptly, and Drakon looked down at me again. Tension thickened the air between us, and his expression softened just briefly. "Good morning."

I wanted him to kiss me so badly that I ached with it. The intensity of my desire scared me.

Maybe that's why I said something stupid. "I expected you to be gone."

His brow lowered and his eyes grew shadowed. "Why would I go?"

Offense echoed in his tone, and I realized I'd hurt him.

"Sorry, that was wrong of me to say." Of course, he wouldn't bail on me. Whatever there was between us, whatever the anger and difficulty, he wouldn't abandon me in the middle of the night. He was planning to sacrifice his own life for me out of the misguided belief that I'd be better off without him. "It's just that this... It's a lot."

He drew in a breath. "It is. And I wish it were easier." He hesitated, as if he were about to say more. Instead, he just said, "We need to go."

He climbed out of bed, gloriously naked. I couldn't help but watch as he walked toward the clothes piled on the floor and tugged them on.

How had I ended up here?

My life had seemed so normal and boring just a month ago.

Now it was crazy. And he was the most unexpected part. I'd never thought life had something this spectacular in store for me.

Spectacular and terrifying.

And short lived if he had anything to say about it.

I wasn't going to let him get his way. I'd convince him we were right for each other. That I truly wanted him.

Doubt tugged at me. If last night hadn't convinced him, I didn't know what would.

Nope. I wasn't going to think such negative thoughts. Anyway, the Black Forest called, and I needed to get a move on.

I climbed out of bed, suddenly shy about my nudity. Fortunately, Drakon was facing away from me as he pulled on his shirt.

Dressing in my previously worn clothes was a bit

unpleasant, but soon I was ready for the day ahead. Together, we left the room and descended the stairs to the main foyer. Though we didn't speak, I felt a new closeness between us.

Or it was my imagination?

A few moments after we arrived, the queen drifted into the room. She inspected us. "Are you ready to go?"

"We are," Drakon said. "Is there anything you can tell us about the forest?"

"Stay wary." She shrugged. "It is ever changing. Dangerous, but welcoming at the same time. I've given you permission to enter, so the monsters should leave you alone. Most of them, at least. You will discover more as you ride."

"Ride?" I frowned. "Ride *what,* exactly?"

"Horses, of course." She looked at me like I was crazy, but I wanted to inform her that she was the crazy one if she thought I was going to ride a horse.

A servant appeared from the shadows and pushed open the main doors. The morning was cloudy and dark as I stared out into the courtyard and spotted two large horses with gleaming black coats.

"Horseback is the fastest and safest way through the forest," the queen said. "The horses know the terrain and how to avoid the tree roots that would snap up and try to grab your legs."

Crap.

Looks like we're riding horses.

"Have you not ridden before?" the queen asked.

"I'm from London. Not exactly a lot of pasture around there."

"Well, now is a good time to learn." She gestured toward the horses. "We've packed saddle bags with a bit of food and water. The rest will be up to you."

"Thank you." Drakon inclined his head. "I am in your debt."

Her eyes glinted with interest. "Are you, now?"

"Don't get any ideas."

"Sure, sure. I suppose I won't get what I really want since you seem to have found your mate, but I'll come up with something." Her gaze drifted over me, both curious and disdainful at once.

I was ready to get the hell out of Romania. With a brief *thank you* to the queen, I strode from the foyer and down the stairs.

My heart pounded as I looked up at the enormous horse. He was easily the biggest one I'd ever seen, and I was pretty sure there were fangs in his mouth. Drakon joined me, and I shot him a sidelong glance. "Are these vampire horses?"

"Demon horses, I think."

"Fantastic. First time on a horse and I get a demonic one."

"He's not much different from a regular horse." Drakon stroked the creature's flank. "Bigger and fiercer, but he'll respond to commands."

"What kind of commands?"

"I'll show you. Let me help you up."

I was almost sure I could get on by myself, but I liked the idea of Drakon touching me, so I just said, "Thanks."

He gripped my waist with strong hands, and I repressed a sigh of pleasure.

Focus.

I put my boot in the stirrup and gripped the saddle. Drakon lifted me, and a moment later, I was sitting on the horse.

"I feel like I'm a mile off the ground." The horse shifted beneath me, and I clung to the saddle.

Oh man, this was going to suck.

Drakon gave me a quick lesson on the reins and different signals the horse would follow, then said, "You'll be fine."

"Sure." I wasn't certain I believed him, but I could pretend.

He gave me one last look, then went to his horse, leaving me alone with mine.

I patted the creature's neck. "Nice horsey."

The demon horse gave an irritated huff and a tiny burst of flame emitted from its mouth.

"Nice demon horse?" I tried again, going for something a little more formal.

The horse made a more contented noise, and I stored the information away for later. He was a more formal creature.

Drakon nudged his horse until the animal was beside me, riding with an effortless grace that made it appear as if he and the horse were one. “Ready?”

I nodded, feeling the queen’s gaze on me. She’d come out onto the steps to watch us set off. I could feel her curiosity burning, and it was clear she wanted to know what I was.

Join the party, lady.

The sturdy gate opened as we neared the fortress wall. As we rode through, a light rain began to fall from the cloudy sky. I gripped the reins with one hand and flipped up my collar with the other.

The horses seemed to know where we wanted to go, because they directed themselves around the fortress wall and toward the rushing river behind. The Black Forest loomed on the other side of the water, the trees looking even bigger than I recalled.

A stone bridge spanned the river, and the hooves of our mounts clip-clopped on the hard surface as we crossed. I looked down at the clear water rushing over boulders. Despite the cloudy day and lack of sun, it seemed to sparkle like diamonds.

Too soon, we were on the other side. Magic radiated from the trees, sending a shiver racing across my skin.

“Stay close to me,” Drakon said as his horse picked up the pace toward the forest.

My mount followed, as if it had understood his

words, and within minutes we were riding through the trees.

It was even darker in here, with a thick mist hanging heavy over the ground. Black tree trunks rose tall on either side of us, expanding out into a canopy that blocked the faint sunlight. Our path was lit by a golden glow that shined between the trees, as if the air were lit by magic.

A threat hung heavy on the air, and I could hear animals rustling in the underbrush. Occasionally, I spotted glowing eyes glaring out at us. Shadow creatures drifted at the edge of my vision.

"Do you know where to go?" Drakon asked.

"Give me a moment." There were no obvious signs, so I closed my eyes and called upon my magic, hoping it would work like it had before.

Instead, I felt something from outside of myself, an extra prickle of magic coming from a distance. I opened my eyes, spotting the faint shadow of a person hovering between the trees about forty feet away.

"Do you see that?" I pointed to it.

Drakon squinted in the figure's direction, a frown creasing his brow. "I see nothing."

The shadow moved, the faint glow drifting through the trees. I nudged my horse with my heel, and the creature picked up the pace. "Come on, we need to follow it."

"What is it?" Drakon said, urging his horse beside mine.

"A figure. Not a living person. More like a ghost."

"Can you tell who it is?"

"No. But I can feel that we need to follow them."

The figure led us through the trees, heading toward something with a singular focus, neither faltering nor looking back. I squinted, but it was impossible to make out any details of our mysterious guide's features or clothing.

As we traveled, I led the way since I was the only one who could see the person. It was difficult at first, but I began to get the hang of directing my mount. All around us, animals rustled in the underbrush. Occasionally, I heard a growl or spotted large, bright eyes staring at us.

Tension tightened my shoulders. It was all I could do to hold onto the horse. If my mount was spooked by a monster, I'd be on my arse in the mud in no time.

Eventually, the sun came out, shining through the trees in bright beams of light that were nearly blinding. I blinked, trying to adjust my vision. The harsh beams of sunlight and the blackened trees were an otherworldly combination and mildly disorienting, and the mingled scents of animals and wet undergrowth only made it stranger.

"Be alert," Drakon said. "Something is stalking us."

12

Mac

I never saw the attack coming. One moment I was riding, the next, a beast was charging toward my mount from the undergrowth. It came from my right side, darting around to attack from behind.

The beast looked like a cross between an alligator and a dog, and the eyes glowed with an unholy fire.

Dark magic. My heart leapt into my throat, and my skin chilled, but my horse seemed oblivious as it trotted along. It was the only reason I managed to stay on my mount, most likely.

I drew my sword, gaze trained on the creature as it leapt high into the air and went for my throat. I sliced out with my blade, the steel glinting in the light as it cut through the monster's belly and severed it in half.

Instead of poofing into dust like other dark magic creatures would, it fell to the ground as two parts. In seconds, the severed halves had regrown into two new, identical beasts. Extra limbs extended outward, along with new heads and tails.

Shit.

"Don't cut them in half!" I shouted to Drakon.

Another beast charged the front of his mount. The horse blew smoke from its nose as it whinnied and pranced. When the creature was close enough, the horse stretched its neck forward and breathed a massive blast of fire on the beast. The monster disappeared in a poof of dark smoke.

Shock sliced through me. Instead of being afraid, the horses attacked.

Holy fates, that was the answer.

I turned back to see the two new monsters chasing my mount. I nudged the horse with one knee and tugged on the reins with the other hand, trying to remember the commands I'd been taught.

"Come on, buddy. Turn around."

The horse spun on a dime, making a quick turn, and spotted the monster. It whinnied like Drakon's horse had, and I heard delight in the sound. Smoke wafted from its nostrils and, as the monster neared, the horse hit it with a jet of fire. The creature shrieked and disappeared in a cloud of gray smoke. Without pausing for a break, the horse obliterated the other beast.

"Just make sure your mount can see the monsters!" I shouted, sheathing my sword in the ether. I'd need both hands to direct the horse. That, and a whole lot of luck.

My heart thundered as I searched the forest for the one who had been leading us toward our destination. In the excitement, I'd forgotten about them.

Finally, I spotted the figure through the trees. They hadn't slowed their forward motion, and we couldn't afford to lose them. I nudged my mount with my heels. "Faster, demon horse. Put the pedal to the metal."

The horse snuffled, as if offended by my car reference, but picked up the pace.

Drakon led the way through the woods, better able to direct his mount. He'd been riding since well before there were cars, and it was obvious in the easy grace and strength of his movements. He and the horse worked as one, with Drakon helping the creature spot the monsters that charged them.

Fortunately, my horse followed Drakon's horse, and I let him take the lead, keeping an eye out for attacking creatures and nudging the horse whenever one appeared. Together, we managed to stay alive as we galloped through the forest, dodging between the trees.

Soon, my thighs ached, and my breathing was coming fast. Riding was no easy task, and the attacking creatures didn't make it any better. Our horses never flagged, though, and with Drakon's efficient navigation, we never lost sight of our guide. We'd killed a dozen of the dark magic creatures before they gave up their attack.

After what felt like eons, the figure ahead of us began to slow. A prickle of recognition raced over my skin.

"I feel like I've been here before," I murmured.

"Perhaps you were, and it's with the rest of your lost memories."

"Maybe." I frowned. "It doesn't feel recent, though. It almost feels like déjà vu. Like I can't tell if it's even real."

"Trust your gut."

The figure had stopped, and anticipation made my heart race. My horse slowed as we approached them, stopping about ten feet away.

The ghostly person faced away from us, but from here it was clear our guide was a woman. She raised a hand over her head and made a sweeping gesture in front of her. Magic sparked, and a small building appeared.

I gasped.

"The tomb," I whispered.

When the figure turned, shock made me nearly fall off my horse.

She looked exactly like me.

"Holy fates," Drakon murmured. "Were you expecting this?"

"No." I nudged the horse, and we slowly approached. She stared up at us, her long hair pulled back behind her head and her simple dress and cloak sweeping the ground. From the style of her garb, she'd lived long ago. "Who are you?"

She stared at me, finally speaking in a faraway voice. "Enter the tomb to find what you seek. It has been waiting for you."

"How, though?"

She repeated the message, verbatim.

Frustration swept through me. "I need more details than that. There's a huge padlock on the door."

It looked just like it had in my dream, but the woman had no answers for me. Her form began to flicker out of existence, and her gaze was blank.

"Wait!" I reached for her. "Don't go."

She didn't so much as twitch.

"I don't think she's real," I said. "More like a shadow of a memory rather than a real ghost."

"She's said what she's been bespelled to say, and she's done," Drakon said.

"So, she's basically a hologram like Princess Leia."

"Princess who?"

"You know. *Star Wars*. She begs Luke Skywalker for help."

A moment later, she disappeared entirely. "Yep. Magical hologram." I jumped down off the horse, managing a mostly graceful landing.

Drakon joined me, dismounting like an Olympic dressage rider. Carefully, I tied the horse's reins to a nearby tree limb. The beast huffed and stamped his hooves, and I petted his strong neck. "Thank you for the ride, you beautiful hell beast."

He snuffled, appearing pleased.

Drakon tied his mount to another tree and went to stand in front of the tomb. He tested the lock, but it didn't budge.

I joined him, staring at the small building that was no larger than a little woodland cottage. The stones used to build it were a beautiful creamy marble that gleamed richly in the faint light.

"The lock is made of bespelled gold," Drakon said. "The choice of metal has kept it from corroding, and the spell has kept it strong. Do you know how to break it?"

"Not yet. But I will." I crouched down to inspect it more closely, hovering my hand over the metal to feel the spell. It sparked against my palm, and I winced. "I definitely don't think we should touch it."

My bloodline.

My mother's words echoed in my head. She hadn't been talking about this place, but I was sure it applied here. A ghostly version of myself had led me here—therefor it was likely that something specific to me would open it.

But what?

"Should you try a bit of blood again?" Drakon asked.

"It's as good an idea as any." I drew my sword from the ether and made a small cut in my hand. Pain stung as I raised my bloody palm to the lock and gripped it tight.

Magic sparked against my flesh, hot and sharp. I winced, yanking my hand back and shaking it. As I'd thought, touching it hurt like hell.

A bloody streak marred the golden lock, which still hung from the door, sealing it tight.

"Not blood, then," Drakon said.

Magic.

The word whispered through my mind.

Once more, I raised my hand and gripped the lock. It was easier than ever to call upon my power, which was good, since gripping the lock still hurt. I fed my power into the lock, feeling the metal vibrate beneath my palm. "I think it's working."

"It is. There's a faint glow to the metal."

I kept going, feeding more magic into it. Perhaps it needed to know who I was, or perhaps it needed magical power to unlock. Either way, I'd give it what it required.

But as the minutes passed, the lock lay still and unchanged. There was still a slight glow to the metal, so my power had done *something*. Just not enough.

"What the hell am I missing?" I muttered. Was I not strong enough?

Or was it not a question of strength?

My dream had made it clear that Drakon needed to be here. Somehow, he was a part of this. I withdrew my hand and turned to him. "You try."

Surprise flashed on his face. "What?"

"I've given it my magic, and it's worked. Part way, at least." The metal still glowed, even though I'd released it. "And now you should try."

He looked at me like I was crazy but approached the door and gripped the lock. I felt his magic flare on the air, and the lock glowed even brighter. A moment later, it snapped open.

I grinned. "See?"

"But why?" He looked at me, confusion creasing his brow. "This is about you, not me."

"I'm not sure it is." We were bound, he and I. More so than I'd realized, and the bond had to be an ancient one. This just proved it. "You're part of this. I don't know how, exactly. But you are."

"All right, then." He looked skeptical but said no more.

I turned to the tomb and removed the lock, then dropped it to the ground. The heavy door swung open with the lightest push, revealing a small, dark room.

A shiver of awareness rushed over me as I stepped into the cool air, allowing my eyes to adjust. When they did, I made out a nearly empty room constructed of slabs of beautiful, gleaming marble, but the only furniture within was a large stone dais. A small box sat atop it.

Drakon joined me. Drawing strength from his presence, I stepped toward the box.

Awareness shivered over me, making my skin go cold and my blood hum through my veins. I couldn't look away from the box—whatever was within would change my life.

As I neared, I was able to make out the details. The box was fashioned of gorgeous slabs of thin, clear crystal that glowed, the seams finished in gold. It was one of the most beautiful things I'd ever seen.

But it was the contents that truly absorbed my attention once I was close enough to see through the crystal.

A blood-red lump lay within, and a shiver raced over my skin.

"A heart." The words rushed out of me on a whisper.

"A human heart," Drakon said.

The heart in the forest had been literal. Holy fates. What was I supposed to do with this?

My pulse raced and my bones ached, as if they knew something I didn't. My hand lifted, though I swore it wasn't a conscious movement. Something seemed to have overtaken me, telling me exactly what to do. Carefully, I raised the lid of the crystal box and gazed at the heart. Even though it appeared to have been here for years, it was still glossy red with blood.

With trembling hands, I lifted the heart from the box. It was warm and slick beneath my hands, but I wasn't disgusted. I probably should be, but I wasn't. Instinct rose within me, the craziest idea flashing into my head.

I couldn't resist it, though.

Slowly, I raised the heart to my chest. My blood roared through my veins as I pressed the heart to my chest. It soaked through my shirt, and the thrill of magic rushed through me.

"Mac?" Drakon's low voice echoed in the silent room, but I ignored him, holding the bloody heart to my chest, right over the place where my own heart thudded against my ribs.

Power rushed through me as the heart glowed brightly. It pulsed with magic, turning pale and ghostly as I stared down at it. Within seconds, it looked just like the ghostly version of myself had. And then it disappeared inside me.

I gasped, magic lighting my body up with fierce sparks of power. My muscles, bones, and blood all went wild, and pure adrenaline rushed through me, making me feel more alive than I ever had.

Knowledge crashed into me, and the world began to spin.

"Mac!"

I heard Drakon's worried voice, and then my vision went dark.

13

Mac

When I opened my eyes, I stood in the forest. The huge black trees rose tall around me, their leaves cutting out the light. The leaves underfoot crunched faintly. Creatures rustled in the underbrush.

"Drakon?" I spun in a circle, searching.

But he was nowhere to be found.

Neither was the tomb, in fact.

And I felt...different.

Very different. Like I was there, but not.

I looked down at my body, almost expecting to see a ghostly glow.

I didn't, but I also didn't look like myself. Though my form was solid, I was wearing a simple white dress. It appeared to be hand sewn, and I knew without a doubt that I was occupying the body of the ghost I'd seen in the forest. More than that, I had the strongest sense that I was hundreds of years in the past. Everything in the forest was different. There were still the same species of trees, but they weren't blackened yet.

Nearby, the sounds of a battle raged with the clanging of swords and the screams of men.

Why was I here?

Witness. Learn.

The words flowed through my mind, followed by understanding. My magic seemed closer to the surface now, more easily accessed. Knowledge filled me.

I would only be here a short time, and I was here to learn.

As the realization hit me, my conscious mind receded, and I became the woman in the forest. Great power rushed through me—godlike power.

All around me, the earth trembled. I felt invincible—like I could tear the world to pieces or create new life with the flick of my hand.

Holy fates—I *was* a god, ancient and powerful.

Mareada was my name, and I was the goddess of creation and knowledge. The two were linked, and I possessed their power. I'd possessed them for a thousand years, walking the earth alone as I'd fulfilled my role as goddess.

The power was like nothing I'd ever felt, so intense

that it nearly took me to my knees. I was capable of almost anything, able to manifest my will to create the reality that I wanted.

I walked toward the battle that I could hear in the distance. I had no idea what it was, but the sound was unmistakable. So, too, was the fact that the noises were waning. The shouts came less often, and I no longer heard the clang of weapons.

I came upon a nearby clearing, and hundreds of bodies came into view. Scattered across the forest floor like refuse, they seeped bright red blood into the earth. There were so *many* of them. It tore at my heart, to witness waste like this. They'd had their lives ahead of them, and yet they'd died on this battlefield fighting a war I knew nothing about. There wasn't a single person left alive, and the sheer tragedy of it made me ache with sadness.

With loneliness.

Dying alone in battle must be one of the worst ways to go—so lonely and cold.

The idea of it dredged up the misery that stalked me every day of my life.

I might be a goddess, capable of incredible things, and yet, I was lonely.

So desperately lonely that it raced through my veins like acid. In a thousand years, I'd never found another like me. Love and companionship had been two privileges that humans had enjoyed, but not me.

I'd tried, but it had never worked. Ancient gods like me were rare in this part of the world. Most had disappeared due to lack of human worship. It had been centuries since I'd seen another being like me. Somehow, I'd outlived them all.

It was more curse than gift.

"So much loss," I murmured as I gazed out over the forest.

The scene before me was too painful to bear. Something swept through me, a crazy desire to attempt something I shouldn't be capable of.

I knelt by a pool of blood next to a young man. There was so much blood. I wished that I could move it back into the bodies of those who had died, mending their wounds, and bringing back to life.

It was a feat that was supposed to be beyond the realm of my abilities.

I could manifest many of my desires, but the ability to manipulate life itself wasn't something I possessed.

Yet I couldn't help but try. The life force and the souls of the men who'd fallen lingered nearby, and I would try to give them a second chance.

I knelt and dipped my fingertips in the pool of blood, pouring magic into it. I had no idea what I was doing. Instinct drove me, a desperate desire to give these men a second chance.

As I worked, magic sparked on the air.

Something was happening.

Excitement thrummed within me.

Perhaps I could bring them back, after all.

I kept going, pouring my magic into the red puddle on the ground, desperate to create some good from this tragedy. To undo it.

But something strange happened.

I could feel the life forces of the men melding into one.

I wasn't bringing them all back, I realized.

I was creating a new being from their mingled souls. They would live again, but as one singular stronger being.

Fear raced through me, along with uncertainty.

Dare I keep going?

But could I truly stop and leave this scene of carnage and loss the way I had found it?

I kept going, pouring more magic into the blood at my feet. The figure of a man began to appear, strong and tall and powerful. Kind and intelligent, different from all the men who had lived before.

The more magic that I poured into the ground, the weaker I grew. I'd never felt true weakness before. My power had protected me from such failings.

And yet now, my head swam, and my shoulders sagged.

Suddenly, I knew—if I was going to complete this and give these lost souls a second chance, it would require all my energy. All my life force.

For this one person to keep living, I would have to die.

Fear raced through me.

Dare I keep going?

This wasn't going the way I'd thought. The process would kill me, sucking away my immortality.

Was I prepared for that?

Was I prepared to stop this?

No.

I couldn't bear it.

I might never get to know the person that I was creating, but I couldn't bear to return to the cold, lonely world knowing that I'd left this unfinished.

It was time for someone else to have a chance. As the faceless form on the ground became more real, I began to drift away.

My heart thundered. Dying was fine, but never knowing this person was enough to make me cry out in pain.

Surely there had to be a way I could know him.

An idea flared. Perhaps there was still a chance.

Reincarnation.

I was capable of that. Hopefully.

If I could reserve just a tiny bit of my own magic, I could come back. I could find him. It might take a millennia, but I was willing to wait.

I would give him all my power, use all my magic, but

save the last bit in my heart. It would stay here in the forest in a tomb I created.

So weak that I could barely stay on my knees, I pressed my hand to the earth, envisioning a small tomb with a crystal box inside, a box big enough to contain my heart. As the man continued to form, his features growing more detailed by the minute, the tomb began to grow up from the earth.

Through bleary vision, I watched as the course of my life changed. As one ended, and another began. It took everything I had to make sure my will was done, and even then, I couldn't be sure that I'd managed it.

Finally, blackness took me.

~

I gasped, returning to myself in the present day. I blinked, my eyes bleary as Drakon appeared above me. I lay on the cold stone ground of the tomb, my head resting on his lap. Shock whitened his face.

"Did you see that?" I gasped.

He nodded, his eyes black with wonder and disbelief. "You tried to save the souls of those who died, and as a result, I was created."

I could hardly fathom it. My mind raced with questions, and my limbs vibrated with shock. Shaking, I scrambled to my knees. It was almost impossible to get my breath.

What I'd just seen...

Holy fates, I'd never guessed.

"It was a thousand years ago," I said. "I lived a thousand years before that. But I was so lonely... I think that influenced who you became. I think, perhaps, it's why we are linked."

"I could feel it." His gaze met mine, stark and grief stricken. "It was like something unlocked inside me and I could feel what you felt."

"Because I gave you my magic."

"And you died before I awoke." He rubbed a hand over his face. "I vaguely recall waking in the forest. But the years afterward are a blur. I was so hungry."

I winced. "I'm so sorry. I didn't know what I was doing, just that I wanted to help. I think the tragedy of the battle influenced who you became. Those men died in battle, amid blood lust and fear."

"And thus, I became a vampire." Darkness flashed on his face. "I'm bad for you, Mac. This proves it."

"Are you joking? Can't you see now that I truly want you? That also influenced what happened back then. I wanted a partner—someone to love. I died to be with you, knowing that I might never be reincarnated to find you."

"But you were, and you are a different person now. The goddess who lived a thousand years ago wanted a partner. *You* live in the modern day where you can find anyone. This version of you locked me away in a tomb for five years. You'd rather torture me than be with me."

I winced, unable to deny the horrible deed, a reminder that I'd done something truly terrible to him.

And I still couldn't remember why I'd done it.

"You don't have your memory from the last few years, do you?" he asked.

"I...don't." Damn it, I hated to admit it.

"If you did, you'd probably do the same thing all over again. Something made you do it, and it's as real as the feelings that led you to create me. Worse, it was *this* version of you that decided you'd rather lock me away than be with me."

Shit, shit, shit. I had no idea how to convince him.

"You're too pure and good, Mac. And I'm... me. You know what I've done. Recently, even. Terrible things, and I can't shackle you to a life with one such as me." The loathing in his eyes made me want to scream.

That was the heart of the issue. It wouldn't matter if I could remember why I'd locked him away, not as long as he felt like this. He believed that he was too evil for me, and I would never be able to convince him otherwise.

But I had to try.

"I know I didn't lock you away to avoid a life with you." I gripped his hands, holding tight. "When I remember why I did it, you'll see."

"But *can* you remember?"

I gestured to the crystal box on the dais next to us. "If

I can remember what happened a thousand years ago, I can remember five years ago. I just need to figure out how."

My father. The knowledge slammed into me. If I could find him, I could remember. The mystery involved my parents.

Drakon shook his head but said nothing.

I decided to take it as a sign that he was willing to give me a chance.

I squeezed his hand once more, opening myself up to him. I needed to know how far the curse had gotten. Pain raced up my arm, and my muscles tightened. Even my heart and lungs seemed to seize up. I gasped.

"Mac? What's wrong?"

"Your curse has advanced so far."

"I'm fine."

"You're not. You need blood."

"No."

"You're worth it, Drakon. I'll prove it to you." With shaking hands, I withdrew my sword from the ether once more and sliced my wrist. Pain flared, and blood welled. I hadn't needed to cut myself—he was conscious and could bite me—but I needed to ignite his hunger.

It flared in his eyes, bright and fierce.

I raised my wrist to his lips. "Drink. You don't have to commit to me for forever, but just drink and buy yourself a little more time. *Please.*"

My voice broke on the last word, and he nodded sharply, his eyes tortured, and gently gripped my wrist.

My heart raced as he lowered his mouth to the cut. Slick warmth covered my skin as his lips and tongue made contact. When his fangs sank into my flesh, pleasure gripped me hard. I gasped, swaying where I knelt.

He wrapped an arm around me, pulling me to his side and supporting me as he drew on my wrist, and the pleasure rushed through me.

I closed my eyes, letting go.

Fates, this felt amazing.

Too soon, it was over.

I opened my eyes, meeting his gaze. The intensity in his eyes made my heart ache. Desperate hope filled me.

"I'll convince you." I cupped his cheek, wishing that he could see himself the way I did. "I'll find my father, remember the last five years, and prove to you that I didn't lock you away because I didn't want to be with you."

"We'll find your answers. Then we'll see." For the briefest moment, it looked like he might kiss me.

Instead, he helped me stand, his touch gentle.

"I'm okay." I drew in a deep breath, standing under my own power, and smiled at him. "Time to get answers."

"Do you know how to find your father?"

I touched my chest. Though I couldn't feel the ghostly heart that had disappeared inside my body, I could feel my increased power. The magic rushed through my veins with the strength of a roaring river.

I closed my eyes, retreating inside myself. If I could go calm and still, understanding would come.

And it did.

My past self was part of me now, and I had her knowledge and her gifts. When I opened my eyes, Drakon was staring at me with silent patience.

"You seem different now," he said. "Surer of yourself."

"I am." I walked toward the crystal box that had held my heart. "I'm still myself, but I have the same knowledge and skills as my past self. I just need to learn to use them properly." I raised a fist and brought it down on the crystal box, shattering it into a dozen pieces.

"What the hell was that for?" Concern echoed in Drakon's voice.

"I'm not losing my mind," I said. "I just need a talisman to help me focus my magic."

"You just *knew* this?"

I nodded. "Knowledge is the most valuable part of my powers. It's why I thought I was a crappy seer all those years—information coming to me, that kind of thing."

"And this talisman will help you focus that new power."

I nodded, picking up one of the crystal shards. As I looked at it, a golden chain appeared, latching to the crystal. I slipped it over my neck, immediately feeling more together. "Now that I've been reunited with my past self, I will grow stronger and be able to use my power more effortlessly. Eventually, I won't need the talisman. But while I'm still learning, having a piece of this place will help me."

"You're magnificent."

Surprise flashed through me, and I looked at him. "Thanks."

He nodded. "I thought you were incredible before, but now that you've come into your full self, it's like looking at the sun."

Wow.

I blinked, tears pricking my eyes.

Whatever self-doubt I'd had washed away at his words. I hoped I could do the same for him.

"Let me find my father."

He nodded, and I closed my eyes, envisioning Ludovic. What a miserable irony that I'd waited a thousand years to be reincarnated only to be reborn to such a horrible man. At least my mother wasn't so bad. A bit weird, but not terrible.

As the image of Ludovic formed in my mind, a phrase followed.

The City of Eternal Shadow.

I gasped and opened my eyes. "I know where he is."

14

Drakon

I stared at Mac, awed by the sight of her. She'd been beautiful before—powerful and sure of herself. Intoxicating, really.

But this new version of her...

It was incredible.

I'd watched as she pressed the glowing heart to her chest and become her full self, become one with the woman she'd once been, and the change had gifted her with more magic and strength than I'd thought one person could have.

A goddess.

Macbeth O'Connell was an actual goddess.

And she'd created me.

All this time, I'd wondered who had done it. Knowing that I'd been created from magic and blood had been almost a tease. It had just made me want to know more.

And now I did.

The magic of this tomb had allowed me to watch as she'd done the job.

It had been surreal.

And now I'd drunk her blood, buying myself more time. I needed to use it to protect her.

"Where's Ludovic?" I asked.

"The City of Eternal Shadow. Have you heard of it?"

"No." I frowned. "Can you get any more details?"

"That's what came to me, but it will be enough. It's a very distinct name. I'm certain we can find it. We should start with Seraphia's library. Can you take me there?"

I nodded. I'd never been inside the Guild City library, but I knew where it was. And if Mac wanted to go, it was the least I could do for her.

She was the reason I existed.

Holy fates, the knowledge threatened to level me. I'd never have guessed that.

She'd tried to undo a horrible scene of death and destruction, resulting in my creation out of darkness. I'd proven it in my first centuries as a vampire.

"Drakon?" She frowned. "Are you okay?"

Bloody hell. I'd drifted away with my morose thoughts. "Yes." When I spoke, my voice was too gruff.

"Let's go. I can take you to Seraphia's library immediately."

"Thanks." She reached her hand out, and I stared at it for the briefest second. She gave me a curious look. "It won't bite."

"Of course." I took her hand, bracing myself for the shock of pleasure that would streak up my arm. It happened every time I touched her, and this time was no different.

Except the feeling was stronger. As if my knowledge of our past intensified our bond. Intensified my feelings for her.

Desperate to get away from her and find a moment to return to myself, I called upon the ether. It pulled us in, spinning us through space until it spit us out on the pavement in front of the Guild City Library.

I let go of her hand immediately, stepping back to get some fresh air that didn't contain her scent. Every second that I spent breathing her in was the best kind of torture, and I'd never get my wits about me if I kept doing it.

She was stealing my sense from me.

"Are you all right?" she asked.

"Of course."

She frowned, her gaze turning suspicious as she looked at me. "Really? Because this is the second time I've had to ask you."

"Of course. Just..." I searched my mind for a reason I

might be acting odd. "Hungry. I should find some food. That's all."

"You need blood? I didn't give you much."

Yes. "No. Food."

I couldn't eat, but I could at least get her something.

She frowned, as if she might not believe me.

"Truly. I'm fine."

"All right. There's a cafe down the way. I'm sure they do takeaway sandwiches."

It was the excuse I needed. The lifeline. "I'll see you into the library, and then I'll go pick something up for us."

"I'll be fine going in. Just head over."

I shook my head, wanting to know she'd be safe inside the building before I left her. Seraphia was a goddess herself—Persephone, Greek goddess of plants. And her mate was Hades, god of the underworld. Alone, she would be good backup for Mac. If Hades were there, they'd have a second god on their side.

"Let's go in." I strode toward the small wooden door.

It was an ancient piece of wood inset with panes of mullioned glass. More diamond-paned windows bracketed the door on either side, and the ancient Tudor exterior made the library look deceptively small. Only those who had been inside knew the truth.

The library door opened easily beneath my grip. It swung silently, revealing the massive interior. I stepped onto the ornate tiled floors, looking up at the domed ceiling above. It soared five stories overhead, concealed from the outside by magic.

Huge bookshelves stretched back into the depths of the library, and the smell of a gently burning fire emitted from the office to my left. A quick glance inside showed Seraphia sitting at the desk next to the little fire. Her mate, Hades, sat in a chair nearby. Dressed for battle in leather armor and a sweeping black cloak, he read an ancient, leather-bound tome.

He turned to me, brows going up.

We'd met a few times before, and I nodded my head in greeting. He nodded back, then returned to the book.

Seraphia looked up, a smile lighting her face. "Mac!"

"Hey. Do you have a minute?" Mac hovered in the doorway to the office.

"Sure thing." Seraphia approached.

"I'll be back shortly." I turned and left, satisfied that she was in good company.

As I left, Mac's gaze burned into my back.

Mac

Drakon left the library as silently as he'd entered, but I felt his departure like a physical loss. The air changed, becoming deathly still when he was gone. It was an unpleasant feeling.

"He left quickly." Seraphia looked toward the door that shut behind him. "Everything okay with you two?"

"Not even close."

"Come on. I'll get you a cup of tea, and we can talk about it." She bustled from the office and headed toward the kitchen.

"I'm afraid I don't have the time. And Drakon is bringing food back."

Seraphia turned. "What's going on?" Her gaze met mine, and she narrowed her eyes. "There's something different about you."

"Yeah, about that..."

She approached, her step slow and her eyes searching. When she neared, she gasped. "Your magic."

"A bit stronger, yeah."

She touched my arm, her jaw slackening. "You're a goddess. What kind?"

"Ancient Romanian." I gave a weak smile. "Goddess of creation and knowledge."

"Wow, two things?"

"They're linked, kind of. I just found out."

"Whew. That's got to be a story."

I gave her the quick rundown, speeding through everything I'd learned, including the information about Drakon.

"You *created* him?" Awe sounded in her voice.

"Kind of. It's not like I imagined him exactly as he is and then he appeared. It was more like I was lonely and wanted someone to love and I was also trying to save a whole bunch of men who died in a battle. It was a bit of a mess, but here we are."

"But then you sacrificed your life for his."

"Yeah. I planned to be reincarnated. It worked out, which is good, so it's not like I died forever." Understatement of the century.

"Just for a thousand years. And he never knew you were the reason for his existence."

"Well, he knows now. And it's gotten weird."

"It was already weird between you two. But we'll fix it. How can I help?"

We needed to find the City of Eternal Shadows, but first, I had a question sitting on the edge of my tongue, desperate for me to ask it.

"How do you do it?" I asked. "Feel worthy of being a goddess, I mean."

She'd learned what she was later in life, just like me. Maybe it was easier if you were born into the role, but it sure didn't feel easy to me.

She blew out a breath. "That's a heavy question."

"Yeah. Feeling pretty heavy right now."

"I don't blame you." She went silent for a moment, clearly searching for the right words. "I guess you don't feel worthy. At least I don't. You just try to *be* worthy. And I think you're more than capable of that."

Her simple words might not be the solution I'd wanted, but they definitely helped. I reached for her hand and squeezed it tight. "Thanks. You're the best."

She smiled. "I try. Now, what are we looking for?"

Mac

It took two hours to find our answers, but without Seraphia, it would have taken two days. Drakon had brought us all sandwiches and tea, and we'd scoured the books she'd pulled from the shelves.

Once I found it, I stared down at the text in front of me. "No surprise, it's in Romania."

Yesterday, I hadn't even known I'd had Romanian ancestry.

Now, I was a freaking *goddess* of the place, and my bastard father all but owned an entire town there.

"I've heard of this town." Drakon pulled the book across the table so that he could look at it. "I didn't realize it was still there, or that it went by the City of Eternal Shadows."

"What do you know of it?" I asked.

"It's a well-fortified magical city that has been ruled by a long line despots for centuries. Your father must be the latest."

“This book says that it’s impossible to enter without the ruler’s explicit permission,” Seraphia said.

“How does he control that?” I asked.

She flipped the pages, her brow creased as she read carefully. “It looks like there’s a barrier that’s linked to his life force. Some kind of spell. As long as he’s in full control of his power, it’s impossible to cross the barrier. When he weakens, so does the barrier.”

“Hmm.” I leaned back in the chair. “There’s no way to break it?”

“Not that I can see in this book.”

I looked at Drakon.

“I hadn’t heard that,” he said. “So, I know nothing of it.”

“Damn.” I chewed on my lip. The only plan I could think of was *not* going to go over well.

“What are you plotting?” Seraphia asked.

Whatever it is, it looks dangerous. Genevieve’s voice sounded from my feet.

I looked down at the badger. “Where did you come from? And how can you tell it looks dangerous?”

She shrugged. *Around. And I can tell because you’ve got your danger face on.*

A small laugh escaped me. “What does that look like?”

I know it when I see it. If you looked in the mirror, you’d see it, too.

“What’s she saying?” Seraphia asked.

I translated, and Seraphia laughed. "You know, I think she's onto something. Your eyes get this glint. What are you planning?"

"If we can't get to him, I need to let him take me."

"Absolutely not." Drakon's voice was hard. "That's not an option."

"It will be fine. I'll be prepared." But still, the idea made me nervous.

"No." His eyes flashed with anger. "It's too dangerous. We'll find another way."

"I make my own decisions." I scowled at him. "If I want to do this, I will."

His jaw clenched. For the briefest moment, he was silent. Then he just said, "Do not do this. Please."

The softness of his voice startled me, but it was the genuine plea in his tone that set me on my ass. He'd never spoken like that before.

I glanced over at Seraphia, whose brows had climbed halfway up her forehead in surprise. She gave a small shrug, which I interpreted as *How can you say no to that?*

I looked down at Genevieve, who was staring at Drakon with mooney eyes. It was clear what she would do.

"We can find another way," he said. "It will be better to approach him with a bigger force. We're more likely to succeed."

He wasn't wrong about that. "All right. Let's think of something then."

"I wonder if the witches can do a locater spell to find him?" Seraphia said.

"It will only help if he's not in his city." I chewed on my lip. "I wonder if we can draw him out?"

"The thing he wants most is you," Drakon said. "But if we make it clear that you're waiting for him on the outskirts of the city, he'll have the power of his entire security force behind him. He'll know it's a trap."

He was right. We'd be giving Ludovic too much time to prepare. We needed something that wouldn't rouse his suspicion, but what?

Then the idea came. "What about a compromise?"

"What kind of compromise?" Suspicion echoed in Drakon's voice.

"He comes to me in my dreams and tries to steal me away. That means we can make contact there. What if I can do something within the dream to weaken him?"

"Too dangerous," Drakon said.

"Didn't you say I start to disappear when he gets ahold of me in the dream?" I could still remember the tug of the ether as Ludovic tried to pull me away.

That's what I saw, Genevieve said.

Drakon nodded reluctantly.

"All right, then. You can be with me while I sleep. If I start to disappear, just wake me. It saved me before."

"I still don't like it."

"That's fine. You just need to tolerate it. I'm meeting you halfway here."

He frowned but said nothing more.

"How are you going to weaken him in the dream?" Seraphia asked.

"I'm not sure. I need to ask Eve. She gave me something to help protect me from him, so maybe there's something that can do this."

"We'll need to be ready to attack, then," Seraphia said. "You'll need to do this in Romania, probably. At the border to the city, so we're ready to strike."

15

Mac

Though Eve wasn't able to help us, we had a backup plan—the Witches' Guild.

"I'm sure they can help," Eve said as we hurried through the streets of Guild City. "They've got a different skill set than I do, and someone in their guild must be able to create a spell that will weaken Ludovic through a dream."

"Fates, I hope so," I muttered, and glanced back over my shoulder.

Drakon followed us, his gaze on me. He'd been unusually silent since we'd arrived back in Guild City, and that was saying something for a man who normally wasn't very talkative.

His gaze flashed as it met mine, though it was impossible to read whatever thoughts he held within. My heart ached just to look at him. Time was running out for us if I couldn't get him to take my blood again. At some point, the idea of losing him had become unbearable.

"You worried?" Eve asked.

"You can tell?"

"Ha. It radiates off you. What are you worried about?"

"Drakon. Myself. The whole of it."

She gripped my hand in a comforting gesture. "We'll fix it. Between the lot of us, we can do anything."

The mention of my friends and their willingness to step in and help boosted my spirits. When we reached the edge of town near the Witches' Guild, I felt my spirits lift even more. We would find help here. I could feel it.

As usual, the ramshackle wooden tower appeared to be listing slightly to the left, and blue smoke rose from the chimney. The grass in front was still dead as a doornail and singed in areas, suggesting a recent disaster with some fireworks.

We made our way toward the tower and climbed the wooden steps to the top. Jeeves, the witches' butler, opened the door before we could knock.

His dour expression became a grimace when he met

my gaze. "Macbeth O'Connell. Not here to cause mischief, I presume."

I honestly didn't have it in me, which was a first. Normally, I lived to play pranks on the witches and annoy Jeeves. "Not today."

He frowned, worry flashing on his face.

I was so surprised that I nearly fell off the stairs. "Jeeves?"

He cleared his throat and stepped back. "You may enter. And may I say that I hope everything is all right."

It was the nicest thing Jeeves had ever said to me, and my eyes pricked with hot tears. In the midst of all the stress, his concern was enough to push me over the edge. Jeeves and I might have been devout enemies, but his words made it clear that deep down, he kind of liked me. At least, a little.

"Thanks." I managed to blink the tears back in my eyes as I stepped over the threshold.

"The witches are in the swimming room."

I nodded and headed down the hall, Eve and Drakon following. After so many years of friendship with the witches, I'd grown familiar with the layout of their tower. It was far bigger on the inside than it appeared to be, and the rooms frequently changed their décor, meaning more than a fresh coat of paint and a jazzy new rug. Take the front parlor, for example. There were usually alligators swimming in a moat around the couches. Today, however, piranhas leapt into the air like synchronized swimmers practicing their routine. The flesh-eating plants that decorated the walls snapped at them, trying to grab a bite.

I loved the witches' tower.

I stole a peek over my shoulder at Drakon and found him looking at the piranhas with interest. From his expression, he didn't love the place—he wasn't the sort to have such strong emotion over a location—but he seemed intrigued.

The sound of shouts came from the far side of the house.

"Must be a party," Eve said.

Nothing new there. The witches were always having parties. Normally, I was invited, but lately, I hadn't even had a chance to check my text message for invitations.

When we reached the pool room, it was clear that every witch in the guild was in attendance. Two dozen people were shoved into the swimming pool, each sitting on a massive raft and drinking a colorful cocktail. On the far wall, an enormous screen showed a movie. The witches laughed and hurled popcorn at the screen, and I winced as some of it fell toward the water. As the popcorn neared the surface, a spell whisked it away into the ether.

"Wow, this looks fab," Eve whispered. "As soon as we're done with Ludovic, we should put a pool in our tower."

"Where, though?"

She shrugged. "We'll ask the witches to do it. I'm sure they can come up with something."

"Works for me." I searched the water for Coraline, Beth, or Mary. The three witches served as the acting leaders of the coven while their true leader, Hecate, was missing. Almost immediately, I spotted Genevieve. She floated on her own raft, a Manhattan clutched in her hand. When we made eye contact, she gave me a toothy grin.

"That badger knows how to find a good time," I muttered.

My gaze finally snagged on Coraline. She floated in the middle of the pool, her dark hair pulled up into high, matching pigtails. Black eye makeup surrounded her eyes, and her lips were painted a brilliant red that matched her bikini.

When she met my gaze, she smiled widely and gestured for us to come in. "The water's great!" she shouted. "So is the movie. Join us."

"Emergency," I said. "Can you help?"

She frowned, then began to paddle toward the side of the pool. Her raft butted up against the others', and she shoved them aside. "Make way, bitches, your queen is coming through."

The other witches laughed and grumbled, throwing popcorn at her. A few bright white kernels stuck to her hair, and she brushed them off before climbing out of the water.

"What's up?" she asked. "You look like someone walked on your grave."

"Yeah, I've got some things going on."

Eve raised a brow. "That's what we're calling you turning into a goddess? *Things?*"

Coraline's dark eyebrows shot toward her hairline, and she looked me up and down. "Holy fates, she's right. Your magic is off the charts. I thought something felt weird, but I assumed it was hot stuff over there."

Drakon, the hot stuff she was talking about, ignored the comment.

Mary and Beth climbed out of the pool, joining Coraline. The three were hardly ever apart, and as the two other witches stopped in front of us, their jaws dropped.

"Whoa, you're different." Mary gave me a once-over, then wrung the water out of her pink hair. "What happened to you?"

"She turned into a goddess," Coraline said.

"You're kidding me." Beth shot me an appreciative look. "That's wild."

"You're telling me. I'm still not used to it."

"Goddess of what?" Coraline asked.

"Can we go somewhere quieter to talk?" I asked. Something funny had happened in the movie and the other witches were howling so loudly that it nearly gave me a headache.

"Sure, sure." Coraline turned and led us to a small,

dark room decorated to look like a club from the 1970s. Fringe and disco balls were plentiful, and as she slid into a cracked leather booth, "Dancing Queen" came on the speaker system.

I sat squished between Drakon and Eve, and the side of my body that touched the vampire came alive with heat.

Beth leaned forward, her dark braids brushing the table. "Spill."

I gave them a quick rundown of what had happened, then finished with my request. "Can you help me incapacitate Ludovic through my dreams?"

The three witches blew out long breaths in unison as they sat back on their bench seat.

"That's some heavy stuff." Mary frowned. "I know I can't do that. You two?"

Coraline and Beth both shook their heads.

"But we might have someone who can," Mary continued. "Her specialty is the dreamworld. There's a lot of magic there, and she's made it her life's work to understand it."

"Is she here?"

Mary nodded. "She'll be peeved we're interrupting movie night, but she'll help."

Hope flared. "We'll pay her."

Coraline grinned. "She'll insist on it. But it'll be worth it because she's damned good. I'll go get her."

She slipped out of the booth and hurried back

toward the pool room. Mary and Beth leaned toward us, looking at Drakon and me, their gazes bright.

"What's your deal?" Mary asked. "Clearly, there's something between you two."

"Mind your business, Mary." Beth scowled at her. "But really, what's your deal?"

"Hypocrite!" Mary pinched Beth. "You just told me to mind my business."

"True. But then I realized I also wanted to know. You two should *clearly* be together. It's written all over you. And yet, you aren't."

"It's complicated," I said.

"It always is." Beth leaned back. "But it's rarely as intense as it is between you two. I can see it just by looking at you."

"I think perhaps that you should take your own advice," Drakon said.

Beth laughed. "And mind my business?"

He nodded.

She laughed again but continued to study us. Finally, she said to me, "You'll wear him down. You may have to sacrifice, but you'll do it."

"Wait, what?" Surprise flashed through me. "Are you a seer?"

"No. Just have a little bit of sight, that's all."

"Sounds like a seer to me," Eve said.

"Well, I'm not. I'm a witch. And I know what I'm talking about."

"Sacrifice what?" I asked.

"She's not sacrificing anything," said Drakon. "And this conversation is over."

I nudged him, annoyed because I wanted to hear more. "Keep going."

"Sorry, boss man is right." Beth smiled. "That's all I know. And Emmy is here."

I could feel her before I saw her, a prickle of magic on the air. She entered the room, a pale woman who glowed with a faint light.

"She's always looked like that," Mary said. "Not sure why, but it's great for fancy dress parties. She once went as a lamp, and it was hilarious."

Coraline and Emmy approached and stopped right in front of the table. "I hear you need some help with a dream," Emmy said, her thick Cockney accent making it clear she'd been born and raised here.

"Yeah." I laid it out, and her head bobbed.

When I finished, she said, "All right. I think I can help. It'll cost you, though."

"Anything," Drakon said. "But it needs to work. *Well.*"

Offense flashed on Emmy's face. "*Everything* I do works well. My spells are always top notch."

"Chill, Emmy," Beth said. "He's just madly in love with Mac and worried about her."

"Oh, shit." Emmy's brows popped up. "Sorry, didn't

clock that. I'm better with the dream world than the real one."

My blood roared through my ears as I listened to the witches talk about Drakon being in love with me.

It was the first time anyone had said the big L-word.

Could it be true?

I looked at him, finding his expression blank but his eyes hot. Annoyance glinted in their depths, but something else, too.

Acknowledgment?

No, that was crazy.

He didn't love me. If he loved me—

What?

I couldn't finish the thought. I had no idea what I'd do if he loved me.

"Well?" Drakon said. "How long will it take to create the spell? Is it possible to craft one that will kill him outright?"

"Unfortunately, no," said Emmy. "Not through a dream, at least. The best I can do is weaken his power. But the spell will work, I promise."

I prayed she was right because we had no other option.

16

Drakon

The witches were insane.

That was obvious from the moment a person saw their tower, and it became even more obvious upon meeting them.

He's just madly in love with Mac.

Their words echoed in my head, and the thing was, they weren't wrong. I'd accepted that I'd fallen for her. She was unlike any other person I'd ever met. Brave, passionate, strong, intelligent.

Perfect.

But *madly* in love? It made me sound like a character from poetry or a romantic novel.

The worst part was, I felt like one.

She made me feel alive after so many centuries of feeling like I was half dead.

The ghostly witch had given us the spell we'd requested, neatly packaged in a glass vial. She'd called it "the Shocker" and told Mac to slam it into Ludovic's body.

Now, we were on our way back to the Shadow Guild's tower. Eve had called all their friends together to come help. I'd called Dorian, the only person who cared enough about me to come.

The group was waiting for us when we arrived at the tower: Beatrix, Carrow, Seraphia, Quinn, and Dorian. We'd decided that stealth would be necessary for sneaking into Ludovic's city once he was incapacitated, so we kept our numbers small. Carrow's, Eve's, and Seraphia's mates wouldn't come unless called for.

As Eve joined her friends in front of the fire, I stuck close to the wall. Mingling had never been my strength. Even that modern word, *mingling*, was irritating.

Mac stepped to the front of the group and updated them on the plan. When she finished, she looked to Seraphia. "Did you find a bed and breakfast on the outskirts of town?"

"I did. But the place is quiet enough that I think some of us should wait here and transport in once you've incapacitated Ludovic. Otherwise, the innkeeper will think it odd to suddenly have so many guests."

Mac nodded. "Good plan. We'll split into two groups."

I moved to stand near Mac. I'd be going with her, of course. There wasn't a chance in hell I'd let her out of my sight.

Until I turned to granite.

When that happened, she'd be on her own. I wouldn't be able to protect her any longer.

Concern twisted my heart.

She had her friends, so she'd never truly be on her own. But would they look after her the way I would?

Damn it, was I trying to justify taking her blood every day to stay alive? That was selfish, and I'd spent too many centuries being selfish. If I were going to do one good thing with my sorry excuse for a life, it would be this.

"Drakon?" Mac's voice cut through my thoughts, and I realized I'd stopped paying attention.

"Are we leaving?" I asked.

"We are. If you still want to come with me, that is."

"Of course." I itched to reach for her, but I resisted.

It turned out that they'd decided just Mac and I would go to the edge of the city. Everyone else would wait, ready with transport charms to join us.

It didn't take long for Mac to ready herself, and within an hour, we walked in silence out to the courtyard to depart.

"Ready?" she asked when we stopped in the middle.

She'd shown me on a map where she wanted to go, and it would be easy to transport us.

"Yes." I reached for her hand and shivered when we made contact. It took everything I had not to pull her toward me and wrap her in my arms.

I called upon the ether and transported us to Romania. When we arrived, the evening was cool and gloomy. The ancient cobblestoned street sloped inward, the cobbles worn down from centuries of use. Lamplight gleamed golden on them, made brighter by the slick sheen of rainwater that covered the road.

There was no one around, which was convenient. Ludovic's protected city was filled entirely with supernaturals, but even the unprotected outskirts were magical. There were no humans to be concerned about, thank fates.

"Let's find the barrier first," Mac murmured. "I want to see if it's as strong as we expect. Maybe we can slip through or break it somehow."

"I can feel it just up ahead."

"Me, too. It prickles."

We strode down the empty street, passing lifeless shops and flats.

"It's mostly abandoned," she murmured.

"People must have moved into the protected city or away to other places. But why?"

"Because Ludovic is a bastard?"

A likely reason.

At the end of the street, we found the barrier. The air sparked with faint, almost invisible magic that pricked fiercely against the skin.

"I'm not getting a good feeling about this," Mac said.

"Neither am I." We were still a dozen feet away, and the magic was so strong that I wanted to turn back.

We barely made it up to the edge, and by the time I did, it felt like a hundred bees were stinging me.

Tears rose in Mac's eyes. "Looks like we aren't going to be able to force our way through. Let's find the B&B."

"Right." If Ludovic was powerful enough to create this barrier, we'd need all our backup anyway.

It didn't take long to find the B&B. It had no name—just an old sign painted with *Bed & Breakfast* that creaked in the wind. It was one of the only buildings in this part of town with the lights on. The structure was ancient, with peeling paint and cracked windows.

"Charming," Mac murmured. "Why do people come here?"

"Awaiting an audience inside the city, I assume."

"Hmm. We'll have to be wary of the innkeeper, then. She might be on staff to alert Ludovic."

As we approached the front door, it swung open to reveal an older woman. Her gray hair was pulled up into a loose knot behind her head, and her floral dress was faded and old. "Can I help you?" she asked in Romanian.

I answered in English for Mac's sake. "We're looking for a room for the night."

"Just one?" she responded in thickly accented English.

I nodded.

"Very well. Come in."

She named her price, and I nodded despite the fact that it was exorbitant for the poor quality of the inn. We followed her inside the house, which smelled faintly of cleaning solution. Though old and worn, it was impeccably clean.

"There's a room at the top of the stairs that is available." She started up the staircase. "Full house tonight."

There was no sign of other guests, and the air felt still and dead.

"She's lying. There's no one else here," Mac whispered against my ear.

A faint shiver raced down my spine, and I tried to ignore it.

The innkeeper pushed open the door to a large, dark room. The bed was a four-poster—technically built for two people, but old enough that it was still tiny. There would be no king-size beds in this accommodation, I was sure.

"Breakfast is at seven." She stepped back to let us enter. "I'll take payment now, however."

I handed her cash, and she counted it carefully. "That will do."

She turned to leave, but Mac spoke. "Just a moment, please."

The woman looked up, surprised as Mac approached. She stopped in front of the woman, making careful eye contact, and her magic flared briefly on the air. "You will forget that we're here. You won't be able to tell anyone."

I'd nearly forgot she had the ability to temporarily erase people's memories. The woman's eyes went blank, and then she shuffled away.

"That should work." Mac turned back to me. "Now I just need to fall asleep." She laughed. "As if that'll be easy now."

"I'll watch out for you."

"I know." Her gaze met mine and softened. She laid a hand on my chest. "How can I convince you that I want you to survive? That I want you to take my blood?"

"You can't."

"Then perhaps I can convince you that I want *you*. Just you." She leaned up and pressed her soft lips to mine.

Shock and heat streaked through me. For the briefest moment, I wanted to resist. I even pulled away.

But she gripped my shoulders, trying to hold me to her.

It would have taken nothing for me to tear away, but in truth, I didn't want to.

If I was going to spend eternity with my soul trapped in granite, I wanted the memory of one night with her.

The thought was enough to unlock my self-control and release me. A low groan tore from my throat as I cupped the back of her head and kissed her. She tasted divine and felt even better, soft and strong at the same time.

"Take me to bed," she whispered against my lips, pressing her body's full length against mine.

I hoisted her into my arms. She wrapped her long legs around my waist, pressing her core against the unbearable hardness that ached for her, then sank her hands into my hair and kissed me fiercely as I carried her to the bed. Anticipation coursed through me as I stopped in front of it and lowered her to the mattress.

She moved gracefully to her knees and stripped out of her clothing so quickly that it made my head spin. One moment, she was wearing her signature flannel shirt and jeans. The next, she was clad only in lacy black undergarments. The contrast between her outer apparel and inner was enough to make my head spin.

"You're so beautiful." My voice was rough as gravel.

"Take off your clothes." Her gaze raced over me, hot enough to burn.

I tore my shirt over my head as her hands went to the waistband of my trousers. She undid the buttons, pressing kisses to my bare chest as she worked.

Unable to help myself, I dropped my head back and

squeezed my eyes shut, trying to maintain control. When her hand gripped my shaft, a shudder ran through me. "Careful," I warned, "or this won't last as long as you like."

"Then we'll do it twice."

We don't have time. But I didn't say it. I wouldn't bring our dangerous future or our enemies into this room. Into this moment.

Soon, her touch had me shaking. I had to pull away, my breath coming fast and my hips moving without my consent.

"My turn," I growled, pulling her toward me and lowering my head to her breasts. I pressed kisses to the soft skin above the lace, undoing the garment with a quick flick of my fingers. "Beautiful," I breathed, taking one of her nipples into my mouth.

She sank her hands into my hair and moaned.

I wanted her to feel as desperate as I did. Carefully, I laid her back on the bed. She pulled me down on top of her, arching up to take me into the cradle of her thighs. A thin layer of lace was all that separated us, and the desire that coursed through me was enough to steal my breath. It almost stole my sense.

At the last minute, I remembered to ask, "Are you protected from pregnancy?"

My healing ability meant that I didn't carry illness, but I couldn't leave her with a babe if I turned to granite. Just the idea of it made longing swell within me, a feeling so unexpected that it rocked my world on its axis.

Mac drew me back to the moment by nodding and pulling me closer to her. “I’m on birth control. Stop stalling.”

A low laugh escaped me, as unexpected as the feeling of longing. “I’m not stalling.”

I pressed kisses to her lips, moving against her softness as pleasure coiled inside me.

She shimmied out of her underpants, and the action was enough to steal the last of my control. When she pulled me to her and my hardness pressed to her softness, my vision went black from the pleasure.

With a moan, she shifted until I sank inside of her. A shudder ran through me.

“Fates, you feel amazing.” I kissed her throat as I began to thrust, instinct taking over. I couldn’t get enough of her.

“Drakon.” She gripped my shoulders and moved her hips in rhythm with mine. Magic sparked around us, and my world narrowed until it was only her.

It took everything I had to hold out until she came, and I followed her immediately, losing myself in the most impossible pleasure.

When it faded, I pulled her into my arms and held her close, never wanting to let her go.

17

Mac

The dream started as mist. I stood in an empty space, surrounded by billowing clouds of white. A shiver ran over my skin as I turned in a circle and peered into the milky gloom.

Memories of my explosive night with Drakon tried to invade the dream. As much as I wanted to live inside them, I couldn't. Not now, when I was in danger.

Was Ludovic here?

Why the hell was *I* here?

Of all the things to dream about, this horror scenario was maybe the worst. The fog was so thick that Ludovic could be only feet from me and I wouldn't know it. The idea was terrifying.

I drew in a steady breath and tried to calm my racing heart so that I could hear more easily without the blood pounding in my ears.

Where the hell was he?

A soft, warm weight clutched at my leg. *I can't sense him.*

Genevieve. She'd come.

As much as I appreciated the backup, fear still raced through me. I kept all of my senses alert, desperately searching for Ludovic. I couldn't afford for him to get the jump on me.

It felt like hours passed before I felt him. His magic rolled through the air, sickening and dark.

Genevieve shivered. *I smell him.*

I drew in a breath and gripped the potion that the witches had given me. The small glass vial would incapacitate him. I could do this.

But as the uneasy feeling strengthened and I began to sense his presence, my limbs grew tingly and weak from anxiety and anticipation. I didn't want to let him get close. Hell, I wanted to run.

But I couldn't. This had to be done.

He's only a few feet away, Genevieve said. *Behind you.*

An icy shiver raced over my skin, and my stomach turned. I barely resisted spinning around or running.

When his hand gripped my arm, I spun to face him, adrenaline pumping through my veins. Shock flashed on his face, but he recovered quickly. The ether began to pull on me as he tried to tear me away.

"Oh no, you don't," I muttered.

"You're coming with me," he hissed.

I fought the pull, stronger than I'd ever been, but not quite strong enough. My heart raced as I slammed the Shocker down onto his shoulder. The glass exploded, and magic shot through him. His eyes widened, and he began to twitch as his power flowed out of him. It sparked through the air, making my skin itch and burn.

A grimace twisted his face. "You can't stop me."

The ether pulled hard at me, seemingly undeterred by the damage I'd done to Ludovic. I resisted with all my might, but it had me in its grip. I struggled, trying to break Ludovic's hold in hopes that would weaken the pull of the ether. The witches' weapon was dampening his magic, but he was still strong.

Fear iced my veins.

Genevieve clambered onto Ludovic's back to attack, but he didn't notice her. There was a wildness to his face —a frantic desperation that seemed to give him extra strength. When Genevieve clawed at his neck, leaving bloody gouges, he didn't so much as flinch.

Her eyes met mine. *He's crazy.*

Heart pounding, I kicked up and into his stomach, trying to break free.

No good.

Drakon. I called out to him with my mind, having no

idea if it would work but praying he could hear us through our connection.

I felt nothing at first, but after a few moments, my struggles seemed to have extra power. The ether's grip weakened. Suddenly, a great force pulled me from Ludovic, and I tumbled out of the dream, yanked away.

When I opened my eyes, Drakon was leaning over me. His face was pale with worry, and his hands raced over my body, checking for injuries.

"Are you all right?" he asked.

"I'm good." I gasped, trying to catch my breath. My heart felt like it was going to beat its way out of my ribcage.

Genevieve appeared on the other side of the room and flopped down in front of the fire. *You should have seen his face. He looked like he was going to explode with rage.*

"Good." I shoved my hair back from my face. "It would be helpful if he did. Save us some effort."

Drakon's gaze darkened as he searched me for further injuries. "Are you sure you're all right?"

"I really am." I touched his cheek. "You saved me."

"I'll always save you."

A sad smile tugged at my mouth. "Not if you allow yourself to turn to granite out of some misguided notion of sparing me."

His gaze shuttered, but I swore that I could see indecision flickering there.

He's caving.

I prayed I was right because I was running out of time.

Drakon

I looked down at Mac, my heart racing. The last five minutes had been pure hell. She'd started thrashing in her sleep, then disappearing.

It had taken all my strength to pull her from the dream, and the idea of failing had stolen my breath.

Fortunately, I'd managed to yank her out, but it had been too close. We dressed in silence, the weight of all that had happened between us. It had been the best night of my life, and I'd be giving up more of that magic if I allowed myself to turn to granite.

But I'd be sacrificing Mac if I didn't.

Would it really be a sacrifice, though? She insisted it wouldn't. Perhaps I should trust her.

"Ready?" She stood by the door, her gaze expectant.

"Yes." I followed her outside.

We walked in silence, leaving the bed and breakfast without alerting the owner. It was still dark, and the others met us in a deeply shadowed alley nearby. They appeared one by one, arriving silently in the cool air.

"How long do we have?" Eve asked. Her pink and silver hair had been pulled back into a black cap to help her blend better.

"I don't know," Mac said. "I just hit him with the witches' weapon, so at least a few minutes. Let's get through the barrier quickly."

The last of our group arrived, giving us a total of eight: myself, Mac, Dorian, Eve, Seraphia, Beatrix, Carrow, and Quinn. We were an unusually large group to be wandering the streets—this wasn't really a party town with bands of revelers going from pub to pub—but we might need the numbers when facing off against Ludovic and his forces.

"This way." Mac turned and led the way through the twisting streets of the little town, finally arriving at the barrier that separated us from Ludovic's city. The barrier still pricked against my skin, but not as badly as before. No one complained as we stepped closer.

Mac pressed her hand to it, wincing as she met resistance in midair. "It's definitely penetrable." She pushed harder, forcing her hand through.

I joined her. A moment later, we stood on the other side, and the others followed.

Mac and I shared a look, then turned to face the empty street. Silent houses bordered the cobbled path, similar to the ones outside. There wasn't a person to be seen or heard.

It felt too good to be true.

"Stay alert." I started down the street, Mac at my side.

The first crossroads that we reached was empty, but the next revealed a man with muddy brown eyes and a bruiser's face. His gaze widened as he took us in. Our modern clothing was substantially different than his old-fashioned style.

I lunged toward him.

"Intruders!" he bellowed before I could reach him.

I leveled him with one swift punch, sending him to the ground, but it was too late.

Demons streamed down the street, all of them dressed in identical crimson uniforms.

"Guards." Mac cursed and drew her sword from the ether.

I charged, darting between them and Mac. She cursed again and ran to join me as I met the six demons in the middle of the road. Her steel flashed as she swiped it across the neck of the nearest one, severing the head in one powerful swoop.

I tore the head off another, and our companions joined us as more demons swarmed into the alley.

Quinn shifted into a golden panther, while Seraphia commanded thick green vines that shot from the earth. She ripped apart one of the demons, while Quinn sank his fangs into another. Carrow and Beatrix threw potion bombs, and I caught sight of a massive white wolf out of the corner of my eye. It had to be Eve, the most powerful wolf of them all—a dire wolf. She tore through the demons with a ferocity that rivaled my own.

Within minutes, we'd defeated the lot of them. Carnage filled the alley, blood seeping into the cobblestones as demon corpses began to disappear, their souls returning to their underworlds. None of our side had been killed, though Eve was treating a few injuries with her healing potions. I hadn't seen her transform, but both she and Quinn were back to normal.

"Let's keep going," I said. "And keep an eye out for any spare clothing. We stick out like sore thumbs. If we could change, we'd blend in more easily."

We set off down the street, our small troupe moving silently. A few streets down, we found a tiny backyard strung with washing lines. Dark cloaks hung from the lines, along with simple trousers and shirts.

"This will work." Mac pulled a cloak on and swept it over her shoulders.

I did the same, and the others dressed in what they could find. A few minutes later, we were all attired in simple, drab garments that would allow us to fit in a bit better.

I looked at Mac. "Any idea which way we should go?"

She closed her eyes, and her magic swelled on the air. It was more powerful than ever, and a moment later, her eyes popped open. "Follow me."

I nodded, and our group trailed after her down the

street. We moved as quietly as cats, avoiding people as we cut through town.

"This place is weird," Mac murmured.

She was right. It was far more ancient than any place I'd been in the last decade, like a city trapped in time. There were parts of Romania that were slower to adopt some modern conveniences, but this place was different. It appeared to be at least several hundred years old. There were no vehicles, and the shop windows didn't contain a single telephone or toaster oven alongside the potions and weapons.

"Do you think the people here realize that the rest of the world exists?" Mac asked.

"That barrier could keep them in as well as out, perhaps," I said.

"Then we need to make sure we kill Ludovic." Her voice was grim, and I couldn't help but agree. Destroying him was the best way to destroy the charm that protected the place and trapped the residents.

"We're getting close to water," Eve said. "I smell it."

A moment later, we reached the end of a narrow alley and were treated to an incredible view of a black castle on a hill. A narrow drawbridge spanned a crevasse. We couldn't see the bottom from there, but I, too, could smell water. It had to be a river.

I stepped toward it, feeling a prickle of magic as I crossed a barrier. *Shite.* "Be alert. I tripped a spell of some kind."

"Demons coming from behind," Dorian announced.

I turned and spotted a horde of demons streaming at us from a large guard tower to our left. There were at least a dozen. Within moments, their numbers had doubled. That bastard Ludovic was well prepared.

"Ludovic will know we're here," Mac said. "We're so close to his tower that he'll have been alerted."

She was right. We needed to keep going.

"I'll take care of them," Quinn said. He transformed and lunged for them in feline form. Dorian followed, along with Carrow and Beatrix. The two women hurled potion bombs with deadly accuracy, taking out demons with acid and stunners.

But there were still so many demons.

"They're going to need backup," Seraphia said. She sprinted into the fray to join them, then stopped in the midst of the battle and raised her hands. Vines shot from the earth and picked up three of the demons, tearing them apart. Our companions formed a barrier between us and the demons who continued to appear.

"They've got this," Eve said. "I'll accompany you."

Leaving them to the fight, we ran toward the bridge and stared up at the castle. It was a dark and dreary thing, with many turrets spearing toward the stormy sky. Lightning struck behind it, and I could hear the sound of crashing waves in the distance.

As we neared the rope bridge, new magic filled the air, putrid and dark.

Ludovic was here. I still couldn't see him, but I could feel him.

I glanced at Mac, whose face had gone pale. She looked at me. "He's arrived. Do you feel him?"

"Yes. But you're stronger than he is. You're a goddess."

She swallowed hard and nodded, never slowing. "Right. Hard to remember sometimes."

I turned to her and gripped her arm, holding her gaze and trying to impress upon her that I was deadly serious. "You are powerful, Macbeth O'Connell. Immensely so. Don't forget that."

Her eyes brightened with emotion, and she nodded. "I won't."

"Good."

We'd reached the edge of the ancient, rickety bridge. It was made of rope and wooden slats and looked remarkably unreliable. I moved to go first and test its strength, but Mac slipped in front of me.

My heart climbed into my throat as I watched her walk across. The bridge swayed wildly, looking even more decrepit. Images of the rope snapping and her falling were enough to make my breath go short. The bridge held, however, and she kept moving across. In the distance, lightning struck behind Ludovic's castle. Stairs wound down from the steep hill upon which it sat, terminating at a pathway that led to the bridge.

I followed her, with Eve bringing up the rear.

The bridge swayed underfoot as we ran, and my stomach pitched when I looked down. I'd never had a problem with heights before, but I'd also never been on a swinging bridge five hundred feet above a rocky river.

"How the hell is it so deep?" Mac shouted over the wind. "The crevasse came out of nowhere."

She was right. This type of topography shouldn't be found in this part of Romania. It must have been created with magic.

Mac picked up her pace, nearly sprinting across as she leapt from slat to slat. I kept my distance, not waiting to put too much weight on the same part of the bridge. She reached the other side about forty feet ahead of me, and something relaxed in my chest when I saw her standing on solid ground.

The feeling was short lived, however.

Ludovic appeared on the stairs leading down from the castle. He was still a hundred yards away, but it was easy to see him when the lightning lit the sky.

The impeccably tailored suit he'd worn when I'd seen him last was gone, replaced by a cloak that flapped in the strong wind. His silver hair was stark against the darkness, gleaming under the flash of lightning.

We were only halfway across when he raised his hands. Even from that distance, I could see the evil smile stretch across his face.

A moment later, the ropes that held the bridge together snapped.

18

Mac

The bridge split underneath Drakon and Eve. Terror like I'd never known shot through me, and every inch of my body went cold.

The riverbed was hundreds of feet below. When they hit, they'd die—even Drakon. If only Seraphia were there, she could have used her vines to carry them to safety.

But she wasn't there, and I was a goddess, too.

There had to be a way to save them.

I had only seconds to act, and the idea of Seraphia's vines was a good one. As goddess of creation, I could manifest my desires. Surely I could create something to save my friends.

I gripped the talisman around my neck and called upon my magic, determined to create a miracle.

The ropes that had held the bridge together were thick and strong. I imagined them reaching out and wrapping around my friends' waists.

As I watched, they stretched out and did as I commanded. The first one caught Eve, and the second grabbed Drakon, snapping around him and yanking him to a stop.

I held my breath as I tried to control their motion, gently moving them toward the cliff wall so they didn't slam into it. The whole thing should have been impossible by the laws of physics, but magic was a law unto itself.

When they dangled against the wall, they began to climb toward me. They had hundreds of feet to go, and I tried to help them by using my magic to draw the vines upward.

"Daughter." The evil voice sounded from behind me, and ice crept up my spine.

I turned, spotting Ludovic descending the stairs toward me. The old stone steps wound between boulders, and he glided down them with an eerie grace, his cloak billowing behind him in the breeze.

Suddenly, understanding struck.

"You broke the bridge," I said. I'd been turned away from the castle, watching my friends. I must have missed his arrival.

A cold smile cut across his face. "We hardly need them spoiling our reunion, do we?"

"It's going to be a short one." I called upon my magic, imagining killing him in a hundred different ways.

Before I could strike, Ludovic flicked his wrist, and demons appeared—over a dozen of them, each dressed in the crimson uniform we'd seen on the ones who'd attacked us in the city. They streamed toward me, cutting me off from Ludovic, who still stood on the stairs above me.

"Why are you so determined to kill me?" I demanded, frustrated by my lack of answers.

"Kill you?" He laughed. "I want to *capture* you. You're too valuable to simply kill."

The demons weren't carrying weapons, I realized.

That wouldn't stop me from trying to kill them.

I drew my sword from the ether. I could use my magic to take them out, but it was a finite resource. I'd need time to recover before I could use it again, and I had to save it for Ludovic.

The first demon who reached me drew a shield from the ether and used it to block my sword. Metal clanged against metal, sending vibrations up my arm.

I ducked low and sliced my blade toward the demon's knees. The steel made contact, and he howled, dropping to the ground.

More demons followed, circling me. There were so

damned many. I was going to have to use my magic.

A second later, Drakon and Eve climbed over the edge of the cliff and sprinted toward me. Drakon moved like lightning, reaching the demons before they could lay a hand on me. He grabbed one and spun it around, tearing the head off before the creature could raise a hand against him.

From behind him, Eve transformed into her dire wolf form. She was huge and beautiful, a beast of such graceful ferocity that she looked like a living work of art.

The demons attacked, going for the kill. Claws flashed and blades glinted under the light. The ones that came after me went much more easily. Capturing was a lot harder than killing, and I used that to my advantage.

I cut them down, one after the other, as I tried to reach Ludovic, but he seemed to have an endless supply of them. Every time we killed enough demons to make a dent, he called upon more.

But finally, I cleared a path.

"I'm coming for you," I said, reaching for the magic that I'd saved.

He smiled broadly and beckoned me forward. I approached, climbing the stairs. As I neared, he slipped to the right and disappeared behind a massive pile of rocks.

"Shit." I raced after him, sparing one last glance for Eve and Drakon.

"Go!" Drakon shouted, tearing the head from a demon who had chased me halfway up the stairs. "We'll keep them off you."

I nodded and turned, running after Ludovic. The boulders that he'd disappeared behind had concealed a path. It wound through the rocky terrain, and I raced after him.

The path circled the base of the castle, long and winding. Ludovic was fast and stayed one step ahead of me. As I ran, the sound of crashing waves increased.

Finally, the path opened up to a cliff at the back of the castle. The land disappeared, plunging downward, and the roar of the waves grew even louder. When lightning cracked the sky, I could see the glow reflected off waves in the distance.

Somehow, Ludovic had built his castle in a place that shouldn't exist. This part of Romania didn't have a sea, and yet, I couldn't deny what was in front of my eyes.

As I moved toward the cliff, I began to feel the intensity of the magic in the air. And the misery. The last time I'd felt something like this, I'd been in Ludovic's creepy cavern full of jars containing the souls of his victims.

My gaze was drawn to the sea, and horror dawned.

There were souls trapped *in* the water. They were powering his magic.

I had to release them. But how?

Kill Ludovic.

The answer came to me on a spark of magic.

If I could kill him, the magic that bound the souls to the sea would dissipate. They would be free.

"Daughter." His voice boomed through the night, and I turned to find him standing on a rocky outcropping about twenty feet away. His cloak billowed in the wind, and his eyes burned with unholy fire. "You've come."

"To kill you, yes." I gripped my talisman and called upon my magic, imagining a new form of attack. Though I still didn't know the true extent of my powers, I was going to try to figure it out here and now.

The magic vibrated through my veins, so strong and sharp that I felt like a live wire. I had to release some of this energy, and I imagined great masses of electricity flying through the air.

I raised a hand, delighted to see it sparking with white light.

Ludovic raised his own hand, but I threw my blast before he could attack. A blast of electricity shot toward him and exploded against his chest, throwing him backward. He slammed into a boulder and slumped to the ground.

It wouldn't be that easy.

I braced myself for his attack. I could feel his power on the air, and it was terrifying. The sea full of souls kept him well fueled.

He jumped to his feet and hurled a sonic boom at

me. The noise blasted through the night, and I dove to the right, narrowly avoiding it. Ludovic was too quick, though. He hurled a second boom almost immediately, and it hit me in the side. The force of the blast threw me, and my insides felt like they'd been put through a meat grinder.

I landed on my back in the dirt, out of breath. Gasping, I stared up at the lightning, trying to gather myself enough to rise. The pain was incredible, but what was worse was the knowledge that my *father* had just thrown that blast at me.

Finally, I scrambled upright, all of my bones aching. "Why are you so horrible?" I screamed, my voice nearly carried away on the wind.

"Horrible?" He laughed, an evil sound. "Whatever makes you say that?"

"You locked my mother away, you bastard. Now you're attacking me."

Surprise flashed on his face. "She's been dead for years. How did you know that?"

Dead? "She's not dead. I just saw her."

Confusion creased his brow. "How?"

"I found her in the tomb on the island at our old estate." Uncertainty filled me. He seemed so sure that she was dead.

"Your mother's familial estate." Derision tarnished his voice. "This is *my* land." He swept his arm to indicate the area around us.

"It's as awful as you are."

His smile was icy cold. With a flick of his wrist, he sent another sonic boom my way. I dodged right, narrowly avoiding it, then sent a blast of electricity back at him.

He darted aside with the swiftness of a man half his age, and the electricity slammed into a rock behind him, fizzling out.

We circled each other as lightning flashed, each of us sending blasts of magic through the air. It was nearly impossible to find an opening to hit him, and most of my shots went into the rocks.

When he managed to land a blow, the force of the sonic boom nearly knocked me unconscious. I lay on the hard ground, pain radiating through me as I stared up at the night sky.

He'd always been a bastard.

The knowledge filled my head, and memories returned. This moment unlocked something in my mind. Maybe it was the sonic boom or the fact that I was face to face with my father—perhaps it was both. But I was beginning to remember.

Fate had randomly assigned them as my parents. I'd been reincarnated into a family of monsters who'd learned what my power was early on. They'd *both* tried to use me, going as far as forcing me to lock up Drakon. They'd have done it themselves, but they'd known he'd have killed them before they could manage it.

I gasped, shock sending me upright. It gave me strength I didn't know I had, and I glared at Ludovic. "You made me lock Drakon in that tomb."

Relief filled me. *I* hadn't been the one to plan the horrible deed, at least. My mother was a mind mage, able to reach people through their thoughts. She'd *brainwashed* me into locking Drakon away. They hadn't just threatened me to force me to do it. When I'd done it, I'd thought it had been for the best.

"Of course we had to get rid of him," Ludovic replied. "You were too valuable to waste. If he were allowed to roam free, you'd have fallen in love with him and left us. But she and I couldn't agree on what to do with you."

"So you locked her away because you were fighting over me?"

"We had a disagreement over how best to use you."

How best to *use me.* Rage exploded. "You had no right."

"I have the right to whatever I have the strength to take."

Disgusting. "Well, that's not me."

He raised a hand that sparked with magic, and I braced myself to dodge. When he launched it through the air, I narrowly avoided it. Immediately, I threw my own blast at him. It didn't hit, and we traded blows two more times before he caught me again.

Pain pinned me to the ground, but I dragged myself

upright. Ludovic was approaching, and I needed to defend myself. Genevieve darted around him, trying to get close enough to attack, but he kept her at bay with smaller versions of the magic that he sent at me.

Lightning cracked overhead as I tried to hit him with another blast of electricity. But he was too fast, anticipating where my blows would land. I avoided the worst of his strikes, but we seemed to have reached a stalemate.

How the hell was I going to get past his guard?

As if he'd read my thoughts, Drakon appeared on an outcropping to my right. He stood between Ludovic and me, his gaze moving between us.

Distraction, he mouthed at me. Then he darted toward my father.

Ludovic turned in time, his eyes widening, then threw a sonic boom toward the vampire. Drakon was too close to dodge and took the hit fully in the chest.

Fear lanced me, but I ignored it and took advantage of the opportunity that Drakon had created for me. Ludovic's guard was down, and this was my chance.

I called upon every ounce of magic that I had in me, reaching deep. With a scream, I hit him with an electric blast so big that he plowed into the rocks and slumped to the ground.

I could feel it when his life force left us. One moment, we were surrounded by incredible evil, and the next, it was gone. The souls that had been trapped in the sea escaped on a terrible scream, roaring toward the sky and disappearing.

Holy fates, I'd just killed him.

I staggered backward.

It had been necessary, but it still felt like hell.

There was no time to dwell on it, though. Drakon was still down.

Heart pounding, I raced for him, stumbling over the rocks. As I neared, I saw him shifting, and relief rushed through me.

I fell to my knees at his side as he sat up. "Are you all right?" I demanded, searching his face for any sign of pain.

He grimaced slightly and nodded. "I'm fine. How are you?"

I threw my arms around him and hugged him tightly. He grunted but wrapped his arms around me as well.

"Are you sure you're all right?" he murmured against my hair.

"I'm fine. He landed a few hits, but he's dead, thank fates."

He pulled back to look at me, concern in his gaze. "Are you—"

Magic cracked on the air, startling us both. We both turned toward the source of the noise, and the breath whooshed out of my lungs when I saw my mother.

19

Mac

She stood only a few yards away. Suddenly, all the *nothingness* that I'd felt when I'd first seen her returned. Now I knew why I hadn't felt the usual daughterly love.

My mother was a monster.

At present, I felt downright antagonistic. Fearful, even. I was shaking slightly, though whether it was from fear or rage, I had no idea.

Drakon and I rose, facing off against her. Genevieve joined us.

As lightning cracked behind her, my mother stood near Ludovic's body, her dress blowing in the wind. She looked solid and alive, as far as I could tell.

"Ludovic lied," I said. "You're not dead."

She smiled broadly. “Because of you, my dear.”

“I don’t think he lied,” Drakon murmured. “Do you feel her magic?”

I felt for her signature and was startled when I discovered that it felt just like Ludovic’s. But that shouldn’t be the case. Magical signatures were like fingerprints, no two the same.

“What did you do?” I demanded, staring at her with confusion. “Your magic feels like Ludovic’s. Did you take it from him? Is that how you’re here?”

“Damn.” She gave me an unexpectedly proud look. “On one hand, it’s annoying that you figured it out. On the other, I'm sure it’s my genes that make you so clever.”

I ignored the words. “What exactly did you do?”

My mother spread her arms wide as lightning struck behind her. She clearly liked the audience, which made sense, considering she’d been alone for years. “A little spell once I knew what he had in store for me. I couldn’t stop him from locking me away. I starved to death in there, you know, trapped in that damned tomb.”

I winced. That sounded terrible. “And then what?”

“I’d linked my life force to his. When he died, I would be reborn.”

Oh, that was dark. The magic required to perform a spell like that was terrible, but I wasn’t surprised she’d managed it.

“It won’t last long, however.” She frowned. ”He gave

me my second chance, but I'll need to take your power to make it permanent." She strolled toward me, a cloud of dark magic rolling around her feet. Evil glinted in her eyes, and her voice was icy. "Give it to me."

I could feel her in my mind, poking around. Trying to manipulate me. Her magic was rare and powerful, and the feel of it made more memories return. She used her power to enter people's minds and force them to do her bidding.

That was why I'd erased my memory.

The realization shocked me. Holy fates, *I'd* erased my own memory. Years ago, I'd realized that as long as I knew her, she could slip inside my mind to control me. I'd had to forget her to find freedom.

"You manipulated me my whole life," I said, horrified. "Used your magic to control me."

"Of course I did." Glee shone in her eyes, but I could see hatred behind it, directed right at me.

"Why do you hate me so much?"

"I didn't used to." She strolled toward me. "You were a useful tool. But after you destroyed my ancestral home, well...let's just say my feelings changed."

"Destroyed your home?" As I said the words, the memory returned.

The catastrophe at Lakeland had been my doing. Holy fates, I hadn't seen that coming. But now that the floodgates of my memory had opened, there was no stopping them.

Shortly after locking Drakon away, I'd broken free of my mother's control. I'd tried to destroy my parents and gain my freedom by destroying Lakeland.

But it hadn't worked—not fully, at least. The magic that I'd used had turned the estate into a wasteland, but they'd both survived.

So I'd had to run.

"I see you're realizing what you did," she said.

"I kept you out of my mind by using magic to forget you," I replied.

She nodded. "It was clever. I could no longer reach you." She *tsk*ed. "I underestimated you. You were willing to forget your entire life to escape us."

She'd been so entwined in my life that I'd had to erase my past and create a new one. Which meant *I'd forgotten Drakon.*

"I had to." My power was too immense to leave it in her hands. She'd have used it to force me to cause death and destruction across the world. I'd seen into her mind and experienced the dark things she'd planned, and I couldn't let that happen.

As soon as I'd realized I couldn't defeat her, I'd used my power to remake myself. It had saved me from her until I'd started to remember my past.

Lightning struck as she prowled toward me, clearly lining up to attack. I kept a wary eye on her as I searched the recesses of my mind, trying to dredge up more memories. I could feel Drakon at my side, alert and ready. He had my back while I tried to get to the bottom of everything, and I couldn't kill her until I had everything I needed. She was the only one who could answer some of my questions.

A faint shadow lingered at the edges of my mind.

"I released Drakon," I murmured.

"Did you, now?" Interest gleamed on her face. "Your father had already locked me away by then. After you destroyed Lakeland and disappeared, we spent years fighting, trying to find you. Eventually, he decided he wanted to do it on his own."

Bastard. But I couldn't think of him now. My mind was uncovering the memories of releasing Drakon.

I'd done it a year ago, in my sleep. Apparently, I'd been haunted by dreams of what I'd done to him. My conscious mind couldn't remember because I'd erased those memories, but my subconscious suffered from the guilt.

It had been enough to allow me to go to him in a daze and open the tomb. I'd left immediately, never seeing him and forgetting what I'd done because of the spell I'd cast on myself. It had been powerful magic that had hidden my true life from my mind.

Nearly all of my questions were answered. Except one. "Ludovic mentioned the Arcane Order. What is it? A secret society you run?"

She laughed. "Of course not. It's the order of the universe. You are part of it, with your godly power. Your father always considered it to be a rival to his own society—he wanted to manipulate the world instead of letting fate take control. But you disappeared before he could do it."

He'd wanted to use me to control the fate of the world. Like my mother. They just couldn't agree on the details.

What monsters.

I called upon my magic, determined to get rid of her once and for all. Though I reached deep, there wasn't much for me to draw from.

Horror dawned. I'd used it all on Ludovic. I'd need more time to recover.

Drakon seemed to recognize the problem. I could feel his fear for me as he stepped between me and my mother.

Her gaze moved to him, bitter and angry. "You," she spat. "You were always the one who would take her from us."

"I would never have been your puppet," I said, stepping out from behind Drakon.

"All the same, it's time for him to die." She raised her hands, grinning. Magic sparked around her hands as she raised them. The delight that gleamed in her eyes was sickening.

With a laugh, she released a massive blast of dark magic right at Drakon. Fear drove me, giving me extra speed as I lunged in front of him to take the blow. I didn't know if I'd survive, but it didn't matter. Instinct drove me now. I had to protect him. I *loved* him.

"No!" His shout was the last thing I heard as the magic plowed into me.

I could feel her magic reacting with the last of the magic inside my soul. I might be running low on power, but I had enough to repel her attack. My magic acted as a mirror, reflecting hers back at her.

The dark cloud that she'd thrown at Drakon hurtled toward her and slammed into her chest.

She screamed as she was thrown into the boulders behind her. I could feel her life force dissipate as her body disappeared, no longer kept here by her spell.

Shocked, I went to my knees.

Free.

I was finally free.

My entire memory had returned, and it made me realize how damned lucky I was.

Drakon appeared in front of me and dropped to his knees in turn. He pulled me into his arms and murmured against my hair, "Why the hell did you do that?"

"Didn't want you to die."

"I'd rather die than have you sacrifice yourself for me."

"You don't really have a choice in the matter." I hugged him tightly, so grateful that he was still here.

He pulled back, his concerned gaze racing over me.

"Are you all right?"

"Yeah. Achy, but fine." My gaze moved to my father's body. We'd have to bury him, but that could be done later. For now, I had one last job to do. I met Drakon's eyes. "You believe me now that I want to be with you forever? I love you, Drakon."

His jaw clenched, and emotion gleamed in his eyes. "You nearly died for me. Her blast would have killed you."

"I know." I swallowed hard, residual fear making me weak. I'd been prepared for that outcome, but thank fates, my magic had saved me.

It meant I had another chance with Drakon.

I tilted my head to the right, keeping my gaze on his. "Please. I want to be with you forever. You need to believe that."

He drew in a shuddery breath. "I love you, Mac. I don't feel worthy of your gift, but I want to be with you forever, too."

I smiled, then pulled his face down to my neck. When his fangs sank into my flesh, pleasure shot through me. He drank briefly, taking just enough. I could feel him healing the same way I felt him turning to granite, and relief rushed through me.

He withdrew his mouth. After he'd licked his lips, I kissed him, joy exploding inside of me. He wrapped his arms around me and kissed me back as the sun began to rise.

EPILOGUE

Mac

A week later, I walked into the Haunted Hound with Drakon.

It had been a full seven days since I'd remembered my entire past and put it behind me. Drakon and I had spent the week holed up together, recuperating from Romania. Despite the misery of what I'd learned about my past, it had been an incredible time together. The rest of our life would be incredible, as far as I could tell.

All of my friends had survived the fight with the demons, thank fates. I wouldn't have been able to live with myself if anyone had died. We were gathering at the Haunted Hound to celebrate life returning to normal, and I couldn't wait to see them.

Drakon and I were the last to arrive. The bar was already crowded with my friends and their mates. As we walked up, the group turned to smile at us. Though it had been a tragedy to learn that my parents were monsters, they weren't my family.

My friends were my family. They'd had my back since I'd moved to Guild City, and they had my back now.

"Finally!" Carrow raised a glass. "Took you long enough."

"What can I say?" I wrapped an arm around Drakon's waist. "I was busy."

Everyone laughed, and Carrow nodded to the dart-boards on the far wall. "Get your drink and come join us."

"Will do."

The group walked toward the boards as Quinn leaned over the bar to take our order. "Wine cooler for you. But what about him?"

"Whiskey will do. Thank you." Drakon smiled, and the sight made my heart warm. He'd been smiling more lately, and it was a pleasure to see.

"Not a problem." Quinn fixed our drinks, then returned and handed them over. As he passed me my wine cooler, he winked. "You're back on shift starting tomorrow. No lollygagging around anymore."

"Lollygagging?" I laughed. "That's what you call it?"

"The last week, at least."

"Okay, that's fair." I hadn't done a bit of work while I'd been convalescing with Drakon, and the Hound needed me back at the till.

I didn't know the details of what the future held in store for me and my vampire, but I knew we'd be facing it together. We'd keep our own places for now, but I had a feeling that would change soon enough. Since there was no way I'd be moving to Romania, I hoped he'd be taking up residence in Guild City.

He leaned close and whispered in my ear, "What has put that smile on your face?"

"Just thinking of you becoming a city boy."

"City *boy*?"

"I suppose you'll never be a boy. But I'd love to have you closer."

"Here?" He raised his brows as he looked around. "You want me to move to Guild City?"

"Wouldn't hate it." I pressed my lips to his neck.

"We'll see." He kissed the top of my head. "I'm not keen on the city, but wherever you are is where I'll be."

"Yeah?"

He leaned back to meet my eyes. "You know I think the sun rises and sets on you, Macbeth O'Connell. I love you more than life."

"And I love you. More than I can say."

"I'll just settle for you saying it frequently, then."

"I'd be delighted to."

Drakon had given up his immortality to be with me,

but the good news was that his life was now linked with mine. We still didn't know if I had an unusually long lifespan as a goddess, but it didn't matter. When our time on earth was up, my magic told me that we'd go to an afterworld of our choosing. Wherever it was, we'd be together.

Carrow caught my gaze from the other side of the pub and waved us over. I looked up at Drakon. "Ready to play darts?"

"Ready to do anything with you."

I smiled and linked my hand in his. Together, we walked toward my friends. My family.

That's it for this adventure, but if you want another story, check out Midnight Moon, the next series.

THANK YOU FOR READING!

I hope you enjoyed reading this book as much as I enjoyed writing it. Reviews are *so* helpful to authors. I really appreciate all reviews, both positive and negative. If you want to leave one, you can do so at Amazon or GoodReads.

ACKNOWLEDGMENTS

Thank you, Ben, for everything. There would be no books without you.

Thank you to Jena O'Connor, Lexi George, and Ash Fitzsimmons for your excellent editing. The book is immensely better because of you!

Thank you to Orina Kafe for the beautiful cover art.

AUTHOR'S NOTE

Hey there! I hope you enjoyed *Kiss Me*. My books feature history and mythology to varying degrees. In *Kiss Me*, the most notable example of this comes from Mac's heart stored in the tomb in the forest.

I've mentioned before that Guild City is inspired by Sigisoara, the town that served as the birthplace for Vlad the Impaler. While on that research trip, I also visited Bran Castle, which is associated with Vlad but was never ruled by him. Our tour guide told the story of Queen Maria's heart. She was the last queen of Romania and upon her death in 1938, her heart was interred (at her wishes) in her *Stella Maris* chapel.

Thank you for reading, and I hope you stick around for the next series!

ABOUT LINSEY

Before becoming a writer, Linsey Hall was a nautical archaeologist who studied shipwrecks from Hawaii and the Yukon to the UK and the Mediterranean. She credits fantasy and historical romances with her love of history and her career as an archaeologist. After a decade of tromping around the globe in search of old bits of stuff that people left lying about, she settled down and started penning her own romance novels. Her Dragon's Gift series draws upon her love of history and the paranormal elements that she can't help but include.

COPYRIGHT

Published by Bonnie Doon Press LLC

Linsey@LinseyHall.com

www.LinseyHall.com

https://www.facebook.com/LinseyHallAuthor

Printed in Great Britain
by Amazon

18099761R00144